*Clarence*
*is a*
*remarkable*
*dog!*

"We'd better call Clarence," said Mother.

Then Uncle Jeffrey noticed I was telephoning. "What are you doing that for?"

"Calling Clarence," I explained.

Uncle Jeffrey's eyes popped.

"Is Clarence there?" I asked. "Well, would you send him home? All right then, in ten minutes." I hung up. "Clarence wants to see the end of the program."

"What program?" asked Uncle Jeffrey.

"Watching television."

"Watching television!" he exploded.

"Clarence enjoys television, Jeffrey," Mother explained. "He's a very intelligent dog."

# CLARENCE THE TV DOG

By **PATRICIA LAUBER**

*Illustrations by Leonard Shortall*

SCHOLASTIC BOOK SERVICES

NEW YORK • TORONTO • LONDON • AUCKLAND • SYDNEY

FOR CLARENCE

who supplied the stories in this book

and helped with the writing by

lying on my papers

chewing my pencils

putting his face in my typewriter

and untying my shoelaces

Some other books by Patricia Lauber
available from Scholastic Book Services:

Clarence Goes to Town
The Friendly Dolphins



15th printing .................................... January 1971

Printed in the U.S.A.

# CONTENTS

## 1. A BATTLE IS WON

IT started out to be a very dull day. Brian, my brother, was in bed with measles. Mother had gone into town for the morning and left me to take care of Brian. This meant mostly running up and down stairs with glasses of ginger ale or fruit juice, picking up bits of puzzle that had fallen to the floor, and going to see if the mail had come.

Finally Brian settled down, listening to the radio, and I curled up in the living room with a book. I hadn't been reading for more than ten minutes when a huge truck rolled into the driveway and a man rang the bell.

I opened the door.

"Logan live here?" he asked.

"Yes."

"Got your television set. Where d'you want it?"

I hadn't known we were getting television. "Are you sure it's ours?"

"Name's Logan, isn't it?"

I nodded.

"Where shall we put it?"

"In the living room, I guess." Perhaps Mother was surprising us.

Two men carried in a big set and busied themselves connecting wires and plugging it in. I stood watching. They put an antenna on top of it.

"You can get an outside antenna later," one of them said to me. "Here's how it works—on-off, volume, picture, channel selection. Got it? Nothing to it. Just sign here."

I signed and they left.

Upstairs the radio blared. Brian hadn't heard the delivery men. I decided to try the set before telling him about the surprise.

No sooner had I reached for the on-off knob than the doorbell rang again. This time I could see the Railway Express truck in the driveway. The driver unloaded a huge crate and carried it carefully to the back door. He gave me a receipt to sign. Then, as he was leaving, he grinned and said, "Be careful of the wild animal when you open that crate."

Should I wait for help? I wondered. Then I decided no—the crate was addressed to me: MISS PATRICIA LOGAN, THE BIRCHES, FAIRPORT, CONN.

Three minutes later I had it open. At first I thought there was nothing inside. Then I saw a tiny, scared puppy sitting in one corner. He cocked his head and looked inquiringly at me with sparkling brown eyes.

An envelope was tacked inside the crate. I opened it and read:

This is Clarence. He will grow up into a big, fierce watchdog to protect the three of you in the country. Meanwhile, Happy Birthday!

Uncle Peter

I forgot completely about the television. Lifting the puppy, I ran upstairs. "Brian!" I called. "See what I've got!"

Brian was sitting propped up in bed in a darkened room. He was ten then and big for his age. Every inch of him was covered with bright red spots which clashed with his red hair. He looked awful.

He turned off the radio and cried, "A puppy! Where'd you get him, Sis?"

"His name is Clarence. Uncle Peter sent him to me. For my birthday."

"But it *isn't* your birthday," Brian complained, clutching the pup. The expression on his face, even under all those spots, said clearly that he thought if anyone was going to get a dog he should be the one. "You were twelve five months ago."

"I know, but Uncle Peter never gets birthdays right. I didn't notice you sending back the catcher's mask and glove just because your birthday was seven months past."

Even if Uncle Peter's presents do come at the wrong time, they are always wonderful. Ever since our father died, all our uncles have taken a special interest in Brian and me. Uncle Peter has appointed himself uncle-in-charge-of-presents.

Clarence was busily making friends with Brian. "Clarence doesn't seem to mind that I'm all spotty."

"He probably thinks you're always that way," I said, taking Clarence back. "Besides, he's sort of spotted himself." Clarence has big blotches of brown and black and white. He shredded a piece of paper on the bed and leaped back from the scraps as though they might bite him.

"Say, Brian," I said, suddenly remembering. "Did you know that Mother had ordered us a TV set?"

"I thought I was the one who ordered it. Did she order one, too?"

"*You* ordered it?"

"Sure," he said. "I kept hearing these offers on the radio—seven days' free trial. No obligation. So I sent for one."

"Is that all right to do?"

"Why not?" he said.

"But you're supposed to be thinking about buying it."

"Well, I am."

"You don't have any money."

"Mother does. Maybe this will convince her we ought — Oops, you'd better take Clarence out!"

I picked up Clarence and ran.

By the time Mother came home, Clarence had explored the whole house, with help getting up and down stairs. He had eaten half of Brian's lamb sandwich and picked out a warm corner of the kitchen for sleeping. Clearly, he had made up his mind to stay. He particularly liked television. He lay good as gold in my lap watching the programs. When something very exciting happened, like a jet taking off, he let out a little bark. Brian couldn't bear being left out, so he sneaked down and joined us.

When Mother walked into the living room, she was speechless with surprise. She finally got her tongue back and said, "Brian! What are you doing up?" Before he could answer she said, "Where did this television set come from?" And without waiting for an answer to that, she said, "And a dog! What else have you done?"

"Nothing," I said in a very small voice.

"What is the meaning of all this?"

Just then a horde of Indians on horseback galloped across our TV screen, uttering war cries. Clarence leaped from my lap and tore around the room barking. Suddenly he stopped. I jumped up and took him out.

When we came back Brian had just finished explaining to Mother about ordering the TV set.

"Absolutely not," Mother said. "The set goes back tomorrow."

"Tomorrow!" Brian cried. "But there's seven days' free trial. And no obligation."

"Brian," Mother was trying to be calm, "it is not fair to the company to send for the set when we have no intention of buying it. And I've explained to you before that we can't afford a set just now."

"But it's only a small down payment now. You pay the rest in easy monthly installments."

"No," Mother said firmly. "The set goes back tomorrow."

Brian looked crushed. He rubbed his eyes furtively with his fists.

"Where did this dog come from?"

"Uncle Peter sent him," I said.

Mother didn't look very pleased, even though I hadn't

sent for a dog and there were no installments to pay. "Peter might have asked first if we wanted a dog."

"Everybody wants a dog," Brian said.

Mother wasn't convinced. "I've got enough to do with you sick in bed and the house to run."

"We'll take care of him," Brian and I said together.

"And I won't be sick much longer. I'll feed him and everything. That is, if Sis will let me," he added, suddenly remembering whose dog Clarence was.

I said, "And anyway, you can't give back my birthday present."

"But it *isn't* your birthday," Mother cried.

"You kept the bathrobe Uncle Peter sent you for your birthday when it wasn't your birthday," Brian argued.

"Well . . ." Mother hesitated.

Clarence, as if he had been following the conversation, chose this moment to make friends with Mother. He left his television program and tried to climb into her lap. She picked him up. Gently he chewed on one of her fingers, then gave it a good licking. He looked at her with soulful eyes.

"He is sort of cute," she admitted. "But the television goes back tomorrow. And Brian, you scoot to bed this instant."

If we could have only one, I certainly preferred Clarence to TV. I said, "What's more, Uncle Peter says Clarence will grow up into a big fierce watchdog to protect us. We need a dog out here."

Mother looked down at Clarence. "I can hardly believe such a tiny puppy will grow up into a big fierce watchdog."

Clarence growled and snapped playfully at the end of her nose.

Mother's lips twitched. "Well, maybe we do need a dog around here again."

I reached out to turn the television off.

"Don't do that, Sis," she said. "Clarence is enjoying the program. He may just as well watch as long as it's here."

She made Clarence a place on an old chair, so he could watch in comfort. "I'll just see what we have for puppies to eat," Mother said.

Clarence, it was clear, had made a conquest.

## 2. A CAT FOR A GUEST

CLARENCE is the friendliest dog I've ever met. I'm not saying that just because he's my dog, but because I think it's true. He loves everybody he meets, and has right from the very beginning.

I don't think any of us really expected Clarence to grow up into a fierce dog. But Brian and I, for a long time, were counting on a big dog. This didn't turn out the way Uncle Peter had said it would either.

Full-grown, Clarence tips the scales at twenty pounds. He stands one foot three inches tall on four paws. Standing on two paws, he can reach three feet off the ground, which is a very handy height for having a look at what is on the dining-room table. But what he lacks in size he makes up for in brains, so it has all worked out very nicely.

However, it was quite a while before we discovered Clarence wasn't going to grow up into a big fierce watchdog. That is why we were worried when the cat came to stay with us—in case our fierce watchdog-to-be might tear the cat into pieces.

Some time before Clarence's arrival, Mother's cousin had written to ask if she might leave her cat with us while she went on a short trip. "I do not want to leave dear Pussy at the veterinary's," she wrote, "because she is used to family life and would be most unhappy. I would not trouble you except that I know you will enjoy having dear Pussy."

To tell the truth, we had forgotten all about dear Pussy's visit until Mother's cousin arrived at our door. "I can't stop," she said, "but here is Pussy. She gets fed twice a day and I'll be back for her in ten days." With that she handed us a black carrying case and left.

All the dog books say you should introduce the dog and cat while holding them and talking to them. So Brian held Clarence on the floor while I opened the case and lifted Pussy out. We had been expecting a small, delicate cat. Instead I lifted out a huge, rangy, striped beast, which snarled and spit at me. Carefully, I set the creature on the floor.

Brian took one look and said, "Pussy heck. That's a cat." So Pussy for the rest of her stay with us was called Cat.

Clarence and Cat looked at each other. Clarence's ears were pricked up, his eyes shining, and his tail wagging. He had never met a cat before. He squirmed to get away from Brian and start making friends. Cat held perfectly still within my hands. We put their noses together. Clarence's tail beat faster. Cat did nothing.

We backed apart and let go of the animals. Clarence

advanced, prancing. Cat waited until he got close. Then she lifted a paw and biffed Clarence on the nose. Clarence yelped and tried to climb up Brian's leg. Brian lifted him. Clarence looked at Cat in hurt surprise. Cat began to wash her face.

Brian put Clarence down. Clarence thought for a moment and then trotted away. He came back with his favorite toy, a squeaking rubber fish. He put Fish on the floor invitingly and crouched beside it.

Cat finished washing her face and strolled over to Fish. She gave it a poke with her paw. Clarence, thinking a game was starting, made a grab for Fish. Cat gave him another clout on the nose and seized Fish. She jumped to a chair and from there to the mantelpiece, taking Fish with her.

"I don't think I'm going to like Cat," Brian said.

"Neither do I," I replied.

Both Brian and I found our dislike of Cat increasing every day. She was so mean to Clarence! She took all his toys—Fish, Ball, Ring—not to play with, but just so he couldn't have them. If she started a game with a ball of string, she wouldn't let him play, and there are few things Clarence enjoys more than tug-of-war with string. She drank his milk as well as her own, and then sneered at his food.

Cat took over the one chair Clarence is allowed on. She even took his bed. This probably hurt Clarence most of all. His bed is four old cushions and an old bedspread. He makes his own bed and he does not like to have anyone else touch it. If Brian or I try to straighten it out, Clarence paws the whole thing apart. Then he pushes the cushions back and digs at the spread until he has it in a snarl on the cushions. That's the way he likes it.

Cat didn't like the bed that way. She amused herself by straightening it out, stamping it down, and sleeping in it. Clarence would stand watching her and whimpering.

What we couldn't get over was the way Clarence never gave up trying to make friends. He would even open the door for Cat. One of our screen doors has no catch and Clarence can open it from the inside by giving it a bang. So if Cat wanted to come in, Clarence would open the door.

One day, after Cat had been with us a week, Brian came into the kitchen in time to see Cat driving Clarence out of his bed. Brian was getting pretty tired of this. He picked Cat up, chucked her into the cellar, and closed the door.

Clarence and Brian and I had a lovely peaceful day until Mother noticed Cat was missing.

"Where's Cat?" she asked.

"I put her in the cellar," Brian confessed.

"That's what we should have done in the beginning," I added.

Now, Mother didn't like Cat any more than we did. But she has very firm ideas about the treatment of guests. Mother believes that no matter how badly a guest behaves you must act as if everything were all right. You needn't ever invite the guest back. But during the time he is in your house you must be polite and pretend not to notice the bad things he does.

To Mother, Cat was a guest. So we were forced to let Cat out of the cellar.

Cat minced her way out, pretending she had gone down there of her own free will. Then, much to our surprise, she started to play with Clarence. She encouraged him to chase her. Then she chased him. Brian and I were almost falling over with astonishment. Had Cat decided to like Clarence? She hadn't, but by the time we learned what Cat was up to, it was too late to stop her.

Letting Clarence chase her, she leaped onto the sofa, which is forbidden to Clarence, and glanced back to see if he was following. He was. Then Cat leaped gracefully onto a small table, balanced neatly on three paws among the ornaments, and jumped to the window sill. Clarence, blundering along the couch, also leaped to the table. Unfortunately, he leaped with much less grace than Cat.

Mother came into the room just as Clarence and the table crashed to the floor. Cat was laughing on the window sill.

"What is the meaning of this?" Mother demanded.

Brian and I tried to explain together that it was Cat's fault. When that didn't work, we said it was partly our fault. Mother knew only what she had seen.

Finally she said, "I don't care whose fault it was. From now on, if Cat is indoors, Clarence goes out. If Cat is out, Clarence comes in. If it's raining or night, Clarence goes in the cellar. Do you understand, both of you?"

It was most unfair. Whose house was it—Clarence's or Cat's? Brian and I agreed secretly that Cat was going to spend most of her time outdoors.

The next afternoon Mother, trying to make up for having been so strict, took Brian and me to the movies. We left Clarence in and Cat out.

When we came back, the house was filled with dogs. Big dogs, small dogs, black dogs, brown dogs, white dogs, spotted dogs were racing around and playing in our house. Every dog who ever came to see Clarence was there, plus a few we'd never seen before.

"Oh, look!" said Brian. "Clarence is having a party! He's let in all his friends."

One dog kept racing up and down the stairs. "That's Taffy," Brian explained to me. "He lives in a one-story house and doesn't have any stairs."

We shooed some dogs out of the hall and went into the kitchen. One of the big dogs had reached down the dog biscuits and a package of cookies. The boxes lay shredded on the floor. "And they've had refreshments," Brian said. We chased five dogs out of the kitchen.

In the living room, two dogs were sleeping on the sofa. A dachshund balanced on his hind legs on the piano bench. With his front paws he experimented with the piano keys. Clarence, who is very musical, was singing.

Half an hour later we had all the dogs out of the house. Brian and I were straightening up when Mother asked, "Where's Cat?"

None of us had seen her.

"Perhaps one of the big dogs ate her," Brian suggested hopefully.

"Brian!" Mother said.

We looked all over for Cat. Finally we found her on top of the refrigerator. When Mother lifted her down, she jumped immediately to the kitchen table and then back to the refrigerator. During the three remaining days she spent with us, she stayed on the refrigerator except for brief trips outdoors. We even had to feed her on the refrigerator. Clarence got back his bed, his chair, and his toys.

When Mother's cousin had finally come for and removed "dear Pussy," Brian and I had a long talk.

"You see," I said, "Mother's way was right. All of us behaved like perfect hosts, and it still came out all right in the end."

"I guess so," Brian agreed. "But Clarence did most of it. He was so friendly all the time and he even had a going-away party for Cat."

Much to our surprise, Mother had a hook put on the screen door that doesn't catch. It didn't seem quite in line with her ideas of hospitality. But she said from now on Clarence could do his entertaining out of doors.

## 3. UNCLE JEFFREY CHANGES HIS MIND

ONE day we received a letter from Uncle Jeffrey saying that he was coming for a visit. Uncle Jeffrey is Dad's brother and every now and then he likes to drop in and make sure we are getting along all right.

There's only one trouble with Uncle Jeffrey. As an old Army officer, he believes in discipline. This means that if he gives an order, you are supposed to obey. At once. What's more, Uncle Jeffrey has very definite ideas about how everyone should behave.

He has all of us quite well trained. That is, all of us except Clarence and Brian. Brian is halfway trained. But when Uncle Jeffrey had met Clarence briefly one afternoon on another visit, he said Clarence was the most undisciplined dog he had ever seen.

Now that Uncle Jeffrey was coming again, Brian and I made a halfhearted attempt to train Clarence a little better. What I mean is, it doesn't seem to matter if a small dog isn't trained very well. It's not like having a Great Dane which insists on sitting on your lap or jumping from one twin bed to another. And if Clarence gets in the way, somebody can always pick him up and put him in the kitchen.

Anyway, Brian and I tried to train him for the visit, but we didn't get far. Clarence thought we were playing some kind of game with him. By the time we got through, we had worked out a few solutions. I would say, "Heel!" and then Brian would step quickly in front of Clarence and try to stay there. It wasn't easy, but Brian is pretty agile. Even so, Mother didn't think we had better show this to Uncle Jeffrey unless we wanted to demonstrate how well trained Brian was.

The night Uncle Jeffrey arrived, Brian was in bed and Clarence was out. We had a pleasant evening, for Uncle Jeffrey didn't have to scold anyone.

Finally Mother said, "We'd better call Clarence."

"Thought you'd finally come to your senses and got rid of Clarence," Uncle Jeffrey said. Then he noticed I was telephoning. "What are you doing that for?"

"Calling Clarence," I explained.

Uncle Jeffrey's eyes popped with surprise. But he didn't have a chance to say anything for just then I got my connection.

"Is Clarence there? Well, would you send him home, please? Oh, it isn't finished? All right then, in ten minutes. Thank you."

"Clarence wants to see the end of the program," I said to Mother.

"Doesn't make any difference. He should come when he's called," Uncle Jeffrey said. Another idea struck him. "What program? What's he doing?"

"Watching television."

"Watching television!" Uncle Jeffrey is a big, tweedy, red-faced man. But now his face started to turn purple.

"Watching television!" he exploded again.

"Clarence enjoys television, Jeffrey," Mother explained quickly. "He's a very intelligent dog."

"He's liked television right from the beginning," I added. "Brian says he's a TV hound."

"Watching television!" Uncle Jeffrey shouted. "What kind of a thing is that for a dog to do? Television is for people. Dogs should be out howling at the moon or sleeping in their kennels."

Clarence doesn't have a kennel. He sleeps either in the kitchen or on the foot of Mother's bed. I didn't think Uncle Jeffrey should be told that.

In a few minutes Clarence banged on the door. He was full of pep and glad to see Uncle Jeffrey. Clarence always enjoys company. He kept trying to jump into Uncle Jeffrey's lap. Uncle Jeffrey kept pushing him off. Clarence thought this was a game. When he tired of jumping, he untied Uncle Jeffrey's shoelaces.

After five minutes, Uncle Jeffrey had had enough. He stood up to got to bed. "Utterly useless," he said. "Never seen such a useless dog in my life. Might as well keep goldfish." Then he clumped upstairs.

Uncle Jeffrey gets up early in the morning.

So does Clarence.

So does Brian.

On this particular morning, Clarence and Brian went to see Uncle Jeffrey. As Mother and I were making breakfast, we could hear muffled shouts, whistling, and thumps upstairs. It sounded like fun. "They are having such a good time," Mother said, "that it seems too bad to disturb them. But go up and tell them breakfast is almost ready, will you, dear?"

When I got upstairs I found Uncle Jeffrey trying to unpack his clothes into neat piles. Clarence was jumping on the piles, snatching something, and racing around the room with it. Brian had brought his drum for Uncle Jeffrey to see. He was beating on it and whistling *Yankee Doodle*.

"Give that back!" Uncle Jeffrey would yell at Clarence.

"Do be quiet!" he would snap at Brian.

No sooner would he get a shirt back from Clarence than Clarence would snatch a tie. And the drum went thump, thump, thump.

"Get them out of here," Uncle Jeffrey roared at me.

"Yes, sir," I said meekly. "Breakfast's almost ready. Come on, Brian. Come on, Clarence."

Uncle Jeffrey had hurt their feelings so badly that Mother had to make scrambled eggs and bacon for Clarence and pancakes for Brian before they began to feel better.

When Uncle Jeffrey came down he was clearly ashamed of himself. He patted Brian and Clarence on the head.

"There, there, boy," he said to Brian.

"Fine day," he said to Clarence.

"Got a nice head, that dog," he said to the room at

large. "Pity he's so small. Fine drum of Brian's, too. Ought to be played on the parade ground."

Everybody began to feel friendly again. Uncle Jeffrey sat down to eat his breakfast, and Brian and Clarence went out.

Before lunch, Brian and Clarence cornered me. "We're sorry," Brian said.

"Sorry for what?"

"For all the bad things we were thinking about Uncle Jeffrey this morning. He wasn't really being mean, was he?"

"No. Grownups just don't seem to like noise first thing in the morning."

"We were being glad to see him," Brian explained. Clarence wagged his tail. "Now we'd like to do something to make up. Clarence has already tried. He found a bone and put it in Uncle Jeffrey's bed as a surprise."

I hoped I would be someplace else if Uncle Jeffrey climbed into his bed and found a nice bone.

"But I took it out," Brian went on, "when Clarence wasn't looking and put it in *his* bed. Probably he'll think Uncle Jeffrey put it there as a surprise."

Mother called us to lunch before we could decide what Brian and Clarence could do to make up. At the table Uncle Jeffrey, much to our surprise, started to talk about Clarence and television. Mother had warned *us* not to bring the subject up again.

"Very interesting thing, that," Uncle Jeffrey said. "What kind of programs does Clarence like?"

"Almost everything. He isn't fussy—"

"Tap dancing is what he likes best," Brian interrupted.

"But he doesn't get a chance to see much of it—"

"Because," said Brian breaking in again, "it excites him and people send him home so their sets won't get broken with Clarence jumping into the screen."

Uncle Jeffrey acted as if this were the most interesting thing he had ever heard. "A real TV dog. Enjoys football, too, I suppose?"

"Clarence hasn't seen much football because the games are played in the afternoon and Mother says we should be outdoors," Brian said, glancing a little resentfully at Mother.

Uncle Jeffrey thought a moment. "Suppose you're quite friendly with the neighbors? The ones who have Clarence in for television."

"I don't even know them, Jeffrey," Mother said.

His face fell.

"The Brundages just moved in a few days ago, and I haven't had a chance to call yet. The people who owned the house before were friends of ours. When they sold their house, they explained to the Brundages that Clarence liked to come in and watch television."

"They're probably awfully nice," I went on. "They let Clarence in all the time."

"Oh," Uncle Jeffrey said. Then he added, "Big Army football game tomorrow. Saw in the morning paper it's going to be televised. Thought if you knew the people I might have a look at it. Doesn't matter, though."

Everyone could see from his face that it did matter.

"We could call up and explain," Brian said helpfully. "I'll do it for you, Uncle Jeffrey, right now." He started to get up.

"Absolutely not!" Uncle Jeffrey barked. "Not going to go barging in on people you haven't even met. Forbid you to call!"

"Yes, sir," Brian said. "I won't telephone."

That evening Clarence stayed home to have a rousing game of ball with us. He tried to include Uncle Jeffrey in the game, but Uncle Jeffrey wouldn't play. "Dog should get his exercise outdoors," he said.

Around nine o'clock the phone rang. It was the Brundages. They'd heard Uncle Jeffrey was visiting us, and they wondered if he would like to watch the Army game.

Uncle Jeffrey's face lighted up. He was very pleased.

The next afternoon Uncle Jeffrey set off down the road. Clarence and Brian and I followed, trotting to keep up.

Presently we came to the house, which had a brand-new sign in front of it: HENRY W. BRUNDAGE. A lady was resting under a maple tree and a man was putting up a croquet set.

The four of us stopped at the fence.

"Hello," said the man. "Are you our neighbors? Yes, you must be. There's our friend Clarence. I'm Henry Brundage."

"Jeffrey Logan," said Uncle Jeffrey thrusting out his hand.

"Brian Logan," said Brian, imitating Uncle Jeffrey.

"We've met, I think," said Mr. Brundage.

"I'm Patricia Logan, only I'm called Sis," I said.

"How do you do?" replied Mr. Brundage. "I'm very glad to meet all of you. And this is my wife."

Mrs. Brundage also shook hands with us. She opened the gate and we filed into the garden.

"This is very kind of you," said Uncle Jeffrey. "I do hope we're not intruding. If you don't want the children to stay, please say so."

"Uncle Jeffrey!" I protested.

"Goodness, no," Mr. Brundage answered. "The more the merrier."

"We don't have television," I said.

"We almost did," Brian explained, "but Mother sent it back."

"Don't chatter," Uncle Jeffrey said.

"I hope you'll forgive the state of our house," Mrs. Brundage said. "We've just arrived and apart from setting up the croquet and plugging in the television we haven't unpacked much."

"Tell you what," Mr. Brundage suggested. "The game won't start for a little while. Mary, why don't you challenge Colonel Logan to a game of croquet. Clarence and the kids and I will warm up the set."

Brian and I sat down on packing cases while Mr. Brundage turned on the television. Clarence rushed around the room investigating boxes and cartons.

"Haven't made much progress since you were last here, eh, Clarence?" our host said.

A picture flickered on the screen and came into focus. Clarence took a front seat and looked intently at the TV.

"And now," said a pretty lady, "we mix in the flour and spices, beat well, and add half a cup of hot water." The camera moved away from her mixing bowl and focused on a close-up of her. Clarence made a little pleased noise and inched nearer the screen. "And," she said, "then we're all ready to pop the cake into—"

Mr. Brundage turned a knob. "Not very interesting," he said. "But don't worry, Clarence, we'll find something else you like."

"And so," boomed a serious, dull-looking man, "I say to you that if a new incinerator is not to be constructed . . ."

Clarence yawned and lay down.

"Don't blame you." Mr. Brundage flicked the knob. "Feel the same way myself. How about this?"

Music and a clicking noise filled the room. On the screen we saw a line of young men tap dancing.

Clarence sat up. His eyes brightened. He let out a yelp of delight and raced madly around the room. The second time around he turned and leaped toward the screen. Mr. Brundage stepped quickly forward and caught him.

"Gosh," he said, "I forgot that Clarence always wants to join the dancers." He turned to another channel. This was a quiz program. Clarence sat down and watched quietly. Every now and then his tail wagged.

At the end of that program, Mr. Brundage called the croquet players for the football game.

This was the first time Clarence had seen football. He was very interested. In the exciting places he jumped into somebody's lap. Whenever Army scored, he barked. He moved close to the screen and backed away. Two or three times he got so excited he ran all over the house. At the quarters and half he rested.

Army won. Uncle Jeffrey was smiling and shaking everyone's hand. He even shook Clarence's paw. "Shows a real appreciation of football," he said approvingly.

The Brundages invited us to come back any time at all. Brian promised to come back the next day.

When we got home Uncle Jeffrey told Mother all about the game. Only one thing was puzzling him. "Very nice people," he said. "But can't understand how they knew I was here." He looked at me. "Did *you* say anything?"

"No, Uncle Jeffrey."

He turned to Brian. "Did you?"

Brian squirmed in his seat. "Well, yes," he admitted. "But I didn't telephone, Uncle Jeffrey, because I promised not to. I went over to see them. I said you were a friend of Clarence's and that you liked television. They said any friend of Clarence's was a friend of theirs."

First Uncle Jeffrey looked mad. Then he looked as if he were going to laugh.

"Well," he said to Clarence. Clarence jumped into Uncle Jeffrey's lap and bit the end of his nose. "Ha, ha," Uncle Jeffrey said. "Cute little fellow. Useful sort, too. Pleased he considers me a friend."

It was the first time I had ever seen a dog in Uncle Jeffrey's lap. He has always told us a dog's place is on the floor—or outdoors. What's more, Clarence was getting white hair all over Uncle Jeffrey's navy-blue suit.

Clarence went and got Ball. As Mother called me from the kitchen, Uncle Jeffrey, Brian, and Clarence had started a three-way game. Clarence looked pleased. He has always found that people enjoy playing with Ball if they will just try.

## 4. WATCHDOG AT WORK

UNCLE JEFFREY was leaving.

"Goodness, Jeffrey," Mother said. "This was certainly a short visit."

"Oh, I'll be back soon—for the hunting season, y'know. Don't want to wear out my welcome. Besides, everything seems to be going very well here."

Uncle Jeffrey really enjoys it if things are going badly. Then he can take over and straighten them out.

"I do think, though," he continued, "that you should have more insurance on this place. You're out here in the country. Easiest thing in the world for a burglar to break in."

"Jeffrey, I feel sure—"

"Quite realize you've got Clarence to protect you," he laughed. "But even so, I'll just ask the insurance agent to stop in and see you."

"Really, Jeffrey, we are perfectly—" Mother was fighting a losing battle.

"No trouble at all. Going right by the office anyway. Well, good-by, all." He stepped into his car and drove off.

"I don't think it's nice of Uncle Jeffrey to make fun of Clarence that way," I said to Mother.

"He'll be sorry," Brian said. "The next time he comes, Clarence will be a great big fierce dog who'll chew him to ribbons."

"I hear George is visiting his grandparents," Mother said, changing the subject. George's grandparents live down the road from us.

"It's funny George hasn't come over, specially since I wrote him about Clarence and how he is going to grow up into a big fierce watchdog," Brian said. Then he shrugged. "Maybe George is having one of his unfriendly times."

"You could go over and see him," Mother suggested. But just then George walked by. With him was a dog, a huge animal with bulging muscles and fanglike teeth. The dog was wearing a spiked collar and lunging on the end of a chain. It was all George could do to hold on to him. George walked slowly past our house and then disappeared down the road.

Brian's eyes popped. For once he was speechless. I couldn't think of anything to say either.

Later that day George came over. "I've left my dog at the house," he told Brian. "We have to keep him chained in the yard. I bet he's the biggest, fiercest, strongest dog in the state."

"What's his name?" I asked.

"Wolf. But he's much fiercer than any wolf. I'm the only one dares go near him. Say, where's that dog you wrote me about, Brian?"

"Clarence is in the house."

"Clarence? What a name for a dog!"

"Uncle Peter named him that. And it's a much better name than that big brute of yours has, George." I felt I was really too grown-up to be quarreling this way with George, but he was making me angry.

"Yah," Brian said. "You wait till Clarence grows up. You won't dare bring your old dog around here any more."

"In a pig's eye," replied George. "Let's see Clarence."

The three of us went into the house. Clarence came dashing from the kitchen, all set to make a new friend.

George didn't seem to see Clarence. He kept looking around the room and talking to us and ignoring our dog.

Clarence went and got Fish. He stood holding it and looking up at George. George paid no attention. Clarence bit Fish gently, so it squeaked. George went on talking, mostly about Wolf.

At last Clarence began to untie George's shoelaces. He tugged hard on one. At this, George looked down.

"Is that your pet squirrel?" Then he gave a fake jump. "Goodness, *that's* not Clarence, is it?" He doubled over with laughter and clutched his stomach. "I was looking for a big fierce dog about this size." He indicated something the size of a pony.

"Clarence isn't full-grown yet," Brian said.

"How old is he?"

"Ten months."

"Oh, boy, did you get stuck!" George laughed. "He'll never be much bigger than that. I better not bring Wolf around here. Wolf loves to eat and Clarence would make a nice mouthful for him."

With that, George went off whistling. Then we heard him say, "Big fierce watchdog, ha, ha, ha!"

I was so angry tears stung my eyes.

"I hate George," Brian said. "Some day I'm going to beat him up."

Usually Mother doesn't like Brian to talk that way. This time she only said, "I had never realized George was such an unpleasant boy."

I picked Clarence up. "Don't you mind, Clarence. You may not be big, but you're smarter than George and Wolf put together." Clarence licked my face and wiggled down. He ran to the front door, sniffed at the bottom crack, and wagged his tail. The bell rang.

It was the insurance man Uncle Jeffrey had sent to see us. Clarence jumped all over him. The man sat down, brushing off dog hairs.

"Playful little fellow, isn't he?" he said, forcing a smile. Clarence undid his shoelaces.

"Take Clarence into the kitchen," Mother said to us. I fixed Clarence's dinner.

"I bet Wolf can't play games," Brian said. "What fun is a big mutt like that?"

"I bet he's not smart enough to watch television."

"And he couldn't have fixed Cat the way Clarence did," Brian went on.

We had just begun to feel better when we heard the insurance man in the hall with Mother.

"Let me know what you decide," he was saying. "Even with a fierce watchdog like yours," he chuckled, "you could still stand some extra protection."

Brian stuck out his tongue in the direction of the hall.

The man went outside, to his car. "Wow, look at that," he called back. "Now there's some real insurance."

We could see George walking Wolf. Wolf was lunging on his chain and drooling. George carelessly dangled a muzzle in one hand. The end of the chain was wrapped around the other.

"Sis, we've got to do something!" Brian cried.

"I know, but what? What can we do to show them?"

"Could we train him to bite?"

"But we don't want a biting dog! We just want one that seems fierce."

Clarence was the only member of the family who wasn't upset and unhappy. He devoted his whole evening to cheering us up with games of Fish and Ball.

As things turned out, Clarence was right not to worry.

While Brian and I were in agony every time George walked Wolf past our house, Clarence just went on being his happy self. But when the time came, well, this is what happened.

The three of us went to the movies one night, leaving Clarence alone in the house. When we came home and turned on the lights, we found a burglar. He was lying unconscious on the floor, his sack of loot in one hand, his flashlight in the other. Clarence was stretched out beside him sound asleep.

While Mother telephoned the police, Brian got his baseball bat and stood guard over the burglar. But the burglar never stirred, even when Clarence licked his face and bit his nose.

Brian could hardly contain himself. "Oh, boy," he said, jumping up and down, "Clarence caught a burglar. Clarence caught a burglar."

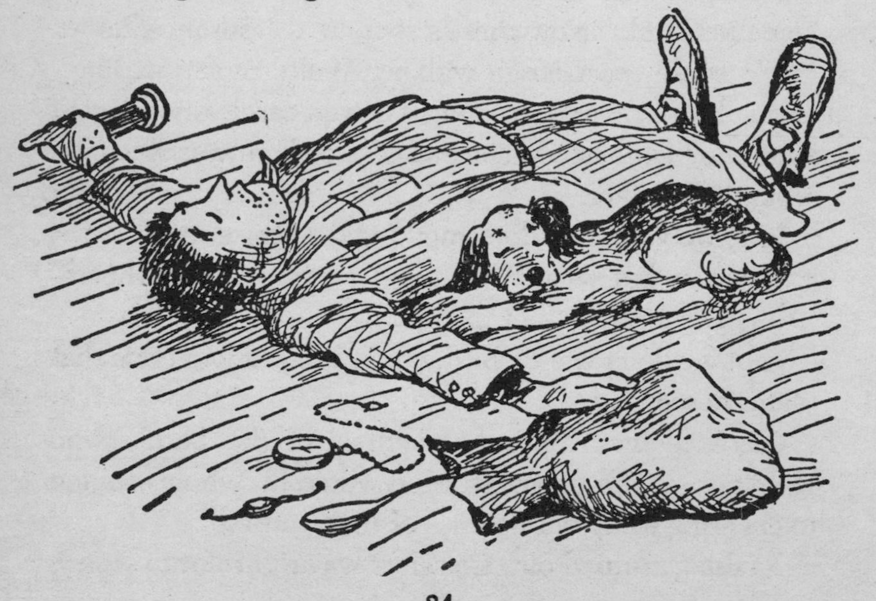

"Just wait till George hears about this," I said. "I can't wait to see his face."

In the excitement, Brian didn't notice Clarence had untied his shoelaces. Hopping around he tripped over one and then skidded on Ball.

Mother came into the room just as Brian was picking himself up.

"What happened?" she cried. "Did that man attack you?"

"No," said Brian. "Clarence tripped me."

We looked around the room. Then we looked at one another. We began to see what had probably happened. Clarence's toys were scattered over the floor. They hadn't been there when we left. So it wasn't hard to see that he had brought them in, hoping to coax the stranger into playing with him. Probably he had started with Fish. The burglar, hard at work, couldn't be bothered. But Clarence had kept on trying, quietly bringing in one toy after another, and expecting the man to like one of them.

Judging from the white dog hair on the man's suit, Clarence had made a try at climbing into his lap and been pushed away. So when all else failed, he had untied the man's shoelaces, and perhaps tugged on one as the man stepped on Ball.

Brian was lucky he hadn't been knocked out, too.

Just as the police arrived, the burglar began to stir. He groaned and rubbed his head. Then he cried out. "Help! Help! Keep them away from me!"

"Here now," Sergeant Murphy said. "What do you think's going on?"

The man looked around. "Protect me, Officer."

"I'll protect you all right. I'm going to put you in a nice safe cell."

"I was attacked," cried the burglar. "I came into this house, thinking it was my own, and was tiptoeing along in the dark, minding my own business, when I was attacked by two armed men and some fierce, bushy-tailed animal."

The police laughed. "You'll have to do better than that," one of them said. Then they took him away, his shoelaces trailing on the ground. "We'll return your property in a little while," one policeman said to Mother.

Sergeant Murphy stayed on to check over the house. Brian and I tagged along at his heels. We had never seen a detective at work before.

Finally, the sergeant told us what he thought had happened. "He broke in here," said Sergeant Murphy, examining a window in the living room. "Then he moved into the dining room to look for your silver. Meanwhile that brave little dog of yours was waiting his chance. When the man bent over, the dog sprang at him and knocked him down in such a way that the burglar hit his head."

Clarence had climbed into the sergeant's lap and was chewing on his uniform buttons. The sergeant patted him. "You're a fine watchdog," he said. "Any time you want to join the police force, just come down and ask for me."

After the sergeant had left, Mother and Brian and I looked at one another. We didn't have to say anything. We were all thinking that we liked the sergeant's account much better than our own.

"Perhaps," I said, "Clarence just happened to take his toys into the dining room."

"And perhaps," said Brian, "the burglar has a dog of his own with white hair."

"And," said Mother, "perhaps he never ties his shoelaces. Some people are very careless about that." She looked at Brian.

But no matter what had happened, we were very proud of Clarence.

We were even prouder the next day when it turned out that our burglar had first robbed the house where George and his grandparents live. Wolf had slept right through the burglary.

Everybody who knew George and Wolf and Clarence laughed over the story. Brian and I biked into town to get a big beef bone for Clarence. We met George in the butcher shop.

George was red in the face and the butcher was saying, "Oh, I've no doubt Wolf, as you say, is a fine fierce watchdog—provided he's not asleep."

George took his parcel and banged out of the shop. The butcher wouldn't let Brian and me pay for the bone. "It's an honor to have Clarence get his bones in my shop," he said. But poor George! His bad day wasn't over yet.

In the late afternoon he came rushing over to our house. "Have you seen Wolf?" he asked. "He broke loose and I've got to catch him before he hurts someone."

"Why, no, George," Mother said kindly. "We haven't seen him, but we'll certainly let you know if we do." All of us felt quite friendly toward George.

Just then I looked out the window. Clarence and Wolf were running round and round the garden, growling.

They say that when you're drowning, your whole life

flashes before you in just a few seconds. Well, that was the way it was with me as I thought, "Perhaps George will do something. Or Mother. Or Brian." Then I thought, "No. Even though Clarence loves everybody and is really a family dog, Uncle Peter gave him to me. So it's up to me to save him." I opened the porch door and stepped out.

I didn't know quite what I was going to do. I looked at the race. It seemed as if Clarence were chasing Wolf. But that couldn't be right. It probably just looked that way because they were going round and round.

I took a step forward. Wolf saw me and dropped out of the race. He bounded toward me. In a flash I saw myself covered with bandages in the hospital. My room was filled with flowers. I wondered if I would get a medal for saving Clarence.

Wolf put his paws on my shoulders and licked my face affectionately. He dropped back to the ground. Clarence dashed at him. Wolf allowed himself to be caught, lay down, and let out pretended moans. Suddenly I realized Clarence and Wolf were having a fine game.

There was a clank behind me. George had dropped the chain and was walking slowly away. The secret was out. Wolf might be bigger than Clarence, but he was not fierce. He was just as friendly as could be once you got to know him.

We didn't see George again for a week, though Wolf came every day to play with Clarence. When Brian and I did see George in town he was telling someone what a fine team our dogs made.

"You don't have to be afraid of burglars around our place," he was saying. "Wolf frightens them, and then Clarence traps them."

## 5. FAME COMES TO OUR HOUSE

FROM the window I could see Clarence and Brian coming back from downtown on Brian's bike. Clarence was riding in the basket, nose pointing into the wind, ears streaming back, and tail blowing in Brian's face. As soon as they reached the house, Clarence hopped out of the basket and dashed off.

"I bet he's gone to the bog again," Brian said in disgust. "I'm getting awful tired of having to wash him."

The bog was Clarence's own discovery. Down the road a new house was being built. Where the workmen had been mixing cement was a big deep puddle. Clarence had taken to bathing in it and coming home covered with mud.

"You know what?" Brian went on. "Clarence has gained two pounds."

"Did you weigh him?"

"Yup and he got a card with his weight and his fortune on it. Wait a minutc." Brian dug into a pocket and brought out a card. He read, "Fate smiles kindly on you. Success is certain in the near future."

"I think the card's behind time," I said. "Clarence has already had his big success, catching the burglar."

Brian added grimly, "And fate isn't going to smile kindly on him if he keeps coming home covered with mud."

Mother came to the door. "Oh, there you are. Will the two of you come and help me set up the folding chairs in the garden?"

"Already?" I said. "But your meeting isn't till tomorrow."

"There'll be a lot to do tomorrow and this is something we can get out of the way ahead of time. I want everything to be just right for the Ladies Club. Miss West is the most important speaker we've had this year, and it's a real honor to be chosen as hostess."

Brian and I didn't think it was such an honor. It meant we would have to get all dressed up and help serve sandwiches and tea. Our afternoon would be ruined.

"While I think of it," Mother continued, "you'll have to keep Clarence in mornings."

"Why?" we asked together.

"Because he goes over to the McLeans' every morning and chases squirrels. Miss West is staying there and she must have quiet for her work. Clarence's barking will disturb her."

"For Pete's sake," Brian said, "she isn't *that* important. I never even heard of her."

Mother stopped unfolding chairs and looked at Brian. "At your age, there are many important persons you have never heard of. Your lack of knowledge does not make them less important. Miss West is one of the leading fabric designers in this country."

"What's that?"

"She makes up patterns for cloth."

"Oh," Brian said.

I hadn't known, either, that people could earn a living doing that. But I was glad Brian had asked the question.

"Right now," Mother said, "she's working on new designs for next spring. Everything must be arranged to make her stay pleasant."

We went on setting up chairs in the garden and arranged the speaker's table. "Pooh," Brian said to me. "I bet she's an old witch. I'll be glad when she goes home."

"We better keep Clarence in, though. If he disturbs her the McLeans will be mad and then Mother will be mad."

Just then Clarence came bouncing back from the bog.

"Down, Clarence!" I said.

Brian sighed. "Is the hose still connected?"

"I think so."

"Come on, Clarence," he said.

Clarence didn't like it when he wasn't allowed to go for his squirrel run the next morning. At first he sulked in his bed. Then he cheered up when he found we were having a party. Parties mean guests, and Clarence loves guests. He ran busily around helping us get ready. He tripped Brian, tore up paper napkins, jumped on the furniture, barked at delivery men, and lay down in a large box of flowers.

Finally, in spite of Clarence, everything was ready.

Brian and I went to get dressed. When we came down, Clarence had disappeared. We looked at each other in dismay. But there was no time to do anything. The guests were already arriving.

Clarence arrived just after Mrs. McLean and Miss West. No sooner had Miss West been seated in the best chair than Clarence burst into the house and jumped into her lap.

"Good heavens!" cried Mrs. McLean.

"Clarence!" Mother said. She sounded just the way she does when Brian or I embarrass her in public.

"Someone remove that animal," Mrs. McLean snapped. "Oh, dear, look what he's done to Miss West's beautiful dress."

Clarence had been in the bog again. At this moment he was standing on Miss West's lap, licking her face affectionately. I lifted him off. Four muddy footprints were stamped on the pale yellow of Miss West's linen dress.

"Gosh, I'm sorry," I said.

"So is Clarence," Brian added. "He didn't mean to do it. He was just being friendly."

Nobody paid any attention to us. Mother and Mrs. McLean had rushed into the kitchen and were coming back with damp cloths. Miss West, who, much to our surprise, was young and pretty, didn't seem upset at all. She was staring thoughtfully at the four prints. When Mrs. McLean began to sponge off the marks, Miss West started to speak but was drowned out by Mrs. McLean. Mrs. McLean had quite a bit to say about children and animals and how they should be kept in their place.

Mother didn't like that, but she just said quietly, "Take Clarence into the kitchen."

I was glad to see that the mud had come off Miss West's dress. She looked a little damp, but I guessed she would dry out.

As we left, Mother was apologizing. Miss West, whom we began to like, was saying it didn't matter at all. Mrs. McLean was glaring at Clarence, Brian, and me.

Half an hour later, Brian came to find me. "Clarence has got into the liver paste sandwiches."

"It's his favorite flavor."

"I know, but what is Mother going to say?"

"She was the one who told us to put him in the kitchen. Where is he now?"

A door banged.

"Oh, oh," Brian said. "He's got out."

We moved quietly into the garden, where the meeting was going on. Clarence had taken a seat in the front row and was listening attentively to Miss West.

"Of course, we all have funny little habits," she was saying. "Mine is that I sing when I'm designing." She turned toward a blackboard, picked up a piece of chalk, and started to sketch patterns.

"Tee-dee-dum," she sang.

Clarence's ears pricked up.

"Dum-tee-tee-dum."

Clarence threw back his head. "Aourrou, aourrou."

"Tiddle-tiddle-dee," sang Miss West, pretending not to notice.

"Aourr-ou-ou-ou."

Mrs. McLean rose from her chair and headed for Clarence. I don't know what she was going to do to him, for Clarence was saved by the unexpected appearance of a young man with a big camera in one hand.

Mrs. McLean quickly changed the expression on her face to a smile. "The press!" she cried. "How nice of the paper to send you. Do take your first photograph of Miss West sketching. It's just too charming."

The young man looked a little bewildered. "I don't know about any Miss West," he said. "Isn't this where Clarence lives?"

"Clarence?" said Mrs. McLean in the tone of a person who has found an old overshoe in the rose bed.

"Yes. Sergeant Murphy told me there was a fine story in how Clarence captured the burglar."

Mother broke in quickly. "Children, do take Clarence and this young man into the house. Miss West, please pardon this disturbance and go on with what you were telling us."

The four of us went inside.

"Gosh," said the young man, "I hope I didn't break up the party."

"Oh, no," I said. "But you saved Clarence from getting into terrible trouble."

"That's nice," said the young man, moving his camera out of Clarence's reach. "How about a few pictures? This won't hurt much, Clarence. Be all over in a few minutes." He focused his camera. "Look alert now."

Brian made a clicking noise. Clarence looked very alert and watchdoggish. The young man snapped the shutter.

As the flashbulb went off Clarence let out a yelp and leaped into my lap.

"What way is that for a brave dog to act?" asked the young man, putting in a new bulb. "Once more now. You can stay where you are."

This time Clarence wasn't so startled. In fact, he decided he liked all this attention. He brought Fish and sat down waiting to be photographed again.

"All right, if you insist," said the young man. He took another photo. "But that's all. If you're a good dog I'll send you a print and you can give it to someone for Christmas."

Clarence took a seat on the sofa and looked hopefully at the young man.

"Absolutely not. Now I'm going to interview you." The young man changed from a photographer to a reporter, bringing out a notebook and pencil. "Let's see. The sergeant told me about the actual burglary. How does Clarence think other homes could best be protected against burglars?"

"If they all had small, brave, alert dogs, they would be safe," Brian said. "They should be careful about getting big dogs. Some of them don't know a burglar when they see one."

The reporter wrote all that down. "Dogs something like Clarence himself?"

"Yes," I said.

"Did Clarence have even a moment of fright when he saw the burglar?"

Brian thought for a minute. "No. Clarence is always

brave, but sometimes he is braver than other times. This time he was very brave."

"Does he expect to make a career out of catching burglars?"

"It's just a hobby, like stamp collecting. If there's a burglar, Clarence will catch him, but he doesn't go looking for them."

"A very sound policy," said the young man. "What are his other hobbies?"

"Well, playing games, doing tricks, watching television."

"And singing," I added.

"And going in bogs," said Brian.

"Brian, do be quiet," I said. "Clarence is my dog. I'll answer for him."

"Well, I guess I can answer, too. Who do you—"

"Ahem," said the reporter. "To get on with the interview. Tell me, to what does Clarence attribute his success?"

"To intelligence," I said. "Clarence saw the problem and tackled it."

"He's much more intelligent than some big dogs around here," Brian added, making a face at me.

"I see." The reporter made a note. "What does Clarence think about the state of the world?"

I replied, "Clarence thinks the world is a lovely place."

"I thought Clarence was just about to get into trouble when I arrived."

"That was because he jumped on Miss West with muddy feet, and ate the liver paste sandwiches, and sang when Miss West did. He was just being sociable," Brian

said. "Mrs. McLean thinks Miss West is more important than Clarence."

"Lots of people around here have never heard of Miss West," I said, determined not to be outdone by Brian, "but everybody knows Clarence."

"Clarence appeals to the masses," Brian nearly shouted, using an expression he had heard someplace.

"In short, Clarence is a local hero and Miss West is trying to crowd him out," said the reporter, scribbling busily. "What does Clarence think of Miss West?"

I said, "Clarence is willing to live and let live. He doesn't mind if Miss West works in our neighborhood. But why should she interfere with his barking and squirrel chasing?"

"Why indeed?" murmured the reporter.

"And Clarence thinks he sings better than she does and she's never caught a burglar," Brian chipped in.

"And the insurance company is giving Clarence a medal for being so brave," I said. "I bet Miss West never got a medal for bravery."

"Now, does Clarence have any words of advice for our readers?" asked the reporter.

"Yes," answered Brian. "Clarence thinks that everyone should be friendly and like dogs and not try to keep dogs out of the fun."

"And Clarence thinks other celebrities should act more the way he does," I said, "modest and friendly."

"That's fine," said the reporter, getting up. "Clarence, it's been a pleasure to meet you. You, too," he said to us. "Must get back now and write up my story."

With that he was gone.

The three of us kept out of sight until the party was over and the guests gone. Then we went out to help Mother clean up. We couldn't tell whether she was annoyed or pleased.

"Clarence certainly did his best to ruin the party," she said finally.

"He didn't *mean* to," Brian said.

"But perhaps now Mrs. McLean realizes she isn't the only one in the neighborhood with a celebrity in the house," Mother continued. She sounded quite pleased, and she didn't say anything about the sandwiches Clarence had eaten.

"I guess maybe the weighing machine was right," I said to Brian. "Fate is smiling kindly on Clarence."

I wasn't so sure about fate the next day when the paper came out. There was a big picture of Clarence on the front page and a long story about him. The story started out fine, with the police telling how brave Clarence was. But for the interview, the reporter had left Brian and me out and just written about what Clarence said and thought. When I saw it all down on paper, it seemed sort of insulting.

I was sure Mrs. McLean and Miss West and maybe even Mother would be furious. Brian thought we should run away from home until the storm blew over. We were sitting in the garden discussing this when Miss West came strolling across the lawn, holding a paper in one hand.

"Now we'll catch it," Brian whispered. "I'm glad Clarence is your dog."

"Hello," Miss West said.

"Hello." We stared at her. She didn't *look* angry, but you can never tell with grownups.

"I'm very sorry to learn that I am the cause of Clarence's being forbidden to chase squirrels," she said gravely, though the corners of her mouth were twitching. "Really, his barking won't disturb me at all."

"Mrs. McLean said it would," I explained.

Miss West sat down beside us. "When I'm working on a good idea, I don't hear anything. And when I run out of ideas—well, then it doesn't matter if there is noise." She looked around. "Where is Clarence? I really came over to thank him."

"*Thank* him?" we said together.

"For jumping on me with muddy feet yesterday."

My mouth fell open. Much as I love Clarence, I certainly wouldn't thank him for getting me all muddy. From the look on Brian's face I could see he thought Miss West was crazy, too.

Hoping to keep Brian from saying anything dreadful, I asked quickly, "You liked it?"

I guess Miss West understood what we were thinking because she laughed. Then she explained, "Clarence's footprints gave me a wonderful new idea. My next designs will be animal prints—dogs, cats, frogs, birds. It was just the kind of idea I'd been trying to find. So I'm very grateful to Clarence."

"Here he comes now," I said.

Clarence trotted around the corner of the house and headed straight for Miss West.

"Watch out!" Brian exclaimed. "He's been in the bog."

Miss West held Clarence off with one hand. "Not today, thanks, Clarence," she said. "Let's not overdo it."

Clarence cocked his head and looked at her. I could see he was still remembering yesterday's disgrace.

Miss West addressed him seriously. "I hope you didn't really think I was trying to steal your glory. I wouldn't do that for anything, Clarence. It's much more important to catch burglars, even as a hobby, than to design patterns. Will you forgive me?"

Clarence's tail wagged.

"And can we be friends?"

His tail wagged even harder.

"And I shall tell all my friends how lucky I was to meet you."

Clarence wiggled all over with pleasure.

"Clarence is honored to meet you, too," I said. "He didn't really mean that you weren't important. He just didn't like being shut in the kitchen."

"Perfectly understandable," said Miss West, getting up. "I shouldn't like to be shut in the kitchen myself."

"Won't you stay for lemonade?" asked Brian.

"Perhaps I could come back another day. I want to work on my new designs this afternoon." She took a few steps, then turned back. "I've told Mrs. McLean that I hope Clarence will visit us. She should be honored that a celebrity wants to chase squirrels on her lawn."

We saw Miss West several times before she left. Later she wrote us that her designs were a big success. Nicest of all, she called them the Clarenzo Prints, which I think is *Clarence* in a foreign language. She sent us samples of the prints and we hung them above Clarence's bed with his burglar medal and his newspaper interview.

## 6. AUNT MINNIE'S RULE BOOK

BRIAN and I went to school, of course. But Clarence didn't. Everything Clarence learned, he just sort of picked up along the way. Nobody ever really tried to educate him until Aunt Minnie came to visit us.

Aunt Minnie is very rich, though you might not think so to look at her. She is tall and thin and papery-looking. She wears straight plain dresses, brown oxfords, and sort of square felt hats. She has a big house of her own, but her husband is dead and her children are grown up. So she spends a lot of her time traveling around, visiting her relatives and giving them advice.

The trouble is, once Aunt Minnie arrives, she doesn't like to leave. She comes to spend a week. Then the week goes by and Aunt Minnie makes no move to leave. She just stays on and on, handing out advice.

Aunt Minnie always carries a book covered with brown paper. By consulting this book she can tell you how to escape from a damaged submarine, how to make elderberry wine, how to make bedroom slippers out of newspaper, and all sorts of things. This would be all right if you needed to know, but Aunt Minnie tells you anyway.

Well, this time she came to see us in September. After she'd been with us three days, Brian took me aside.

"You know what, Sis?" he asked. "Aunt Minnie's talking about Thanksgiving already."

I just looked at him.

"I heard her," he insisted. "She was telling Mother how to preserve the pumpkins from Halloween and make Thanksgiving pie."

"But she can't stay that long. Uncle Jeffrey's coming and we need the guest room."

"Besides which," Brian said, "if she stays that long Clarence and I are going to leave home. We're tired of being poked with her umbrella."

Just then Aunt Minnie came along. "Well, well, young people, what are you whispering about?" she said, playfully poking Brian with the umbrella she always carries because she says you never know when it might rain. Flipping open her book, she read, "One of the first rules of etiquette is never to whisper in corners. Nothing should be said which cannot be heard by all."

She looked at us expectantly. What were we to do? If we told the truth we would be impolite and hurt her feelings. If we didn't hurt her feelings we would have to lie.

Clarence saved us. He came trotting around the corner of the house carrying something in his mouth. Quickly Aunt Minnie reversed her umbrella and hooked his collar with the handle. Clarence's mouth fell open in surprise and a beef bone fell to the ground. Aunt Minnie looked at it approvingly. Still holding Clarence she turned a few pages of her book and read, "Dogs should never be given chicken bones or other small bones which they can easily splinter as these may injure the stomach."

"But Clarence has a beef bone," Brian said.

Raising her voice slightly, Aunt Minnie went on, "It is also inadvisable to feed a dog nuts, since he cannot digest these." Ten minutes later she finished the section on the feeding of dogs, released Clarence, and turned back to Brian.

She read, "Young people should be seen and not heard. They should under no circumstances interrupt their elders."

When I was sure she had finished, I said, "I think Mother is calling me, Aunt Minnie."

"I shall accompany you, Patricia," she said. Thereupon she reached out and ripped a button off my jacket. "Loose," she explained. "A stitch in time saves nine, you know. Page 242," she added.

The button hadn't been loose at all. I just hadn't sewed it on very neatly the last time.

In the kitchen Aunt Minnie took a horrified look at Clarence's bed, which was in its usual jumbled state, just the way he likes it.

"That dog! Every morning I make his bed up neatly with hospital corners and he tears it apart again. Clarence!" she called out the door.

Clarence came warily in, keeping out of range of the umbrella.

Aunt Minnie opened her book and addressed him. "A

bed should be neatly made for the day, coverlet drawn tight. This may be done by forming what are called hospital corners, see illustration, page 102." She thrust the book under Clarence's nose. "Now," she said, "I shall make this bed once more and then you are to leave it alone."

She made it up carefully. Clarence whimpered and made a dive for his bed. "Back!" Aunt Minnie cried, waving her umbrella.

And that was the way it went. All of us were instructed at mealtimes on how to repair clocks, the proper way to row a boat, and how to trap elephants. We had our grammar corrected, our posture corrected, and our table manners improved.

Aunt Minnie also worked on each of us individually. She decided that I was not behaving as a young lady should. I was spending too much time roughhousing with Brian and Clarence. No young lady of twelve should be climbing trees. Aunt Minnie set out to make me over.

She examined me the way one might look over a horse before buying him. I had to walk the length of the room while Aunt Minnie made suggestions about how I should hold myself, and how long my steps should be. She peered at my teeth, suggested that long brown hair was better than short brown hair, and insisted that I spend two hours a day learning how to do embroidery. While I sewed, Aunt Minnie read to me from her book.

Clarence came in for a good deal of lecturing, too. Of course, it wasn't so bad for him because he didn't understand most of what she said. Aunt Minnie felt there was hope for Clarence. He is an excellent listener. He would

sit in front of her, head cocked intelligently, listening to every word she said about how to behave in a dog show, how his coat should be taken care of, how to get rid of worms, and what to do in case of fire.

Sometimes Aunt Minnie held Clarence up to Brian and me as a good example. "If you would only listen as carefully and politely as Clarence, you would learn a good deal more." Brian and I usually squirmed in our chairs trying to think of an excuse for leaving the room. "Do sit up straight!" she would cry, giving each of us a poke with her umbrella.

At the end of the week, Aunt Minnie decided to stay on a little longer. "I shall rearrange my schedule because there is so much to be done here," she said to Mother. "I'm not criticizing, my dear, but I know it is impossible for you to run this house by yourself and train the children and Clarence."

"It's very kind of you," Mother began, "but—"

"Oh, don't thank me," Aunt Minnie said, "I'm happy to be able to do my little bit to help you. I can see the improvement already. All three of them are more subdued. One is hardly aware they are in the house."

This was true. Brian and Clarence and I had taken to gliding around the house so that Aunt Minnie wouldn't know where we were.

Brian and I met behind the barn that afternoon.

"What can we do?" I wailed. "I hate doing embroidery. And I don't want to put my hair up in curlers every night. And I'm black and blue from being poked."

"You should talk," Brian answered. "You aren't being threatened with cod liver oil. She isn't buying long woolen underwear for you. And she isn't enrolling you in dancing school."

"I already know how to dance."

"Well, I don't want to learn. It's sappy."

The back door slammed and Clarence came whimpering over to us.

"She's made his bed again," Brian said.

"There *must* be a way to get rid of her," I said.

"We could put toads in her bed. Or we could send her threatening letters signed 'The Black Gang.' "

"I don't think Mother would like that. You know how she is about guests. Besides, Aunt Minnie means well. She thinks she's being helpful."

"Well, what can we do then?"

"I know." Inspiration seized me. "Let's get hold of Aunt Minnie's book. If we can find out what the title is, we could get copies."

"What good would that do?"

"If Aunt Minnie opens her book and says, 'Too many cooks spoil the broth,' then we can open ours and say, 'Many hands make light work.' "

Brian's face lighted up. "That's a swell idea."

The only problem was how to get hold of the book. Aunt Minnie never seemed to put it down anywhere. We decided to use Clarence as bait. The three of us went into the house.

"Aunt Minnie," Brian said, "could you show Clarence again how he should stand if he ever goes to a dog show and the judges come to look at him?"

"Why certainly. Is Clarence thinking of going to a dog show?"

"Well, he might. I mean, you never know."

"Very true," said Aunt Minnie. "Come here, Clarence."

Clarence looked reproachfully at us. Aunt Minnie laid down her book, her pocketbook, and her umbrella. She tried to make Clarence stand stretched out, head, ears, and tail up. I edged close to the book. Just as my hand touched it, Aunt Minnie turned suddenly. "Hand me my book, please, so I can show Clarence a picture of how he should look."

The plan had failed.

We tried again. While Aunt Minnie worked with Clarence and I stood by, Brian sneaked away into the kitchen. Clarence's bed was just as Aunt Minnie had left it. Brian messed it up the way Clarence does. Then he came back and said, "Aunt Minnie, Clarence's bed is all messed up again."

Aunt Minnie flew into the kitchen. She scolded poor Clarence and laid down her book and pocketbook. She leaned her umbrella against the table. Then she began to make Clarence's bed again. Clarence growled and whimpered. Brian reached for the book. Clarence backed into the umbrella and it fell to the floor with a bang.

Aunt Minnie jumped. "Mercy!" She looked around. Brian had drawn back just in time and was glaring at Clarence.

We made one more try. "Aunt Minnie," I said, "when you get through with the bed, could you show us again how Clarence should lie quietly at my feet on command?"

Aunt Minnie beamed. "I am so pleased that you children *want* to learn now."

We had to carry Clarence into the living room. He was tired of all his lessons.

Again Aunt Minnie laid down her possessions. She busied herself with Clarence, who thought he was supposed to do Dead Dog.

"No, no, Clarence," Aunt Minnie said. "Not like that."

As she bent over him, Clarence spied a handkerchief sticking out of her pocket. He jumped to his feet, snatched it, and retreated backward, facing Aunt Minnie.

"Clarence," she said, "that is not a gentlemanly way to act. Return that to me immediately." As Aunt Minnie advanced, Clarence backed away, tail wagging. "See if you can catch me," he seemed to say.

The two of them disappeared into the hall. We sprang on the book and opened it. Together we flipped over pages, then let the cover fall shut. It wasn't a regular book at all. It was a sort of scrapbook Aunt Minnie had made. She had pasted in clippings and written other things in longhand. We could never hope to get such a book unless we made one, and that would take too long.

Aunt Minnie and Clarence came back to find Brian and me slumped in despair. She poked both of us with her umbrella and said, "Heads up. Backs straight. Feet flat on the floor. As the twig is bent, the bough's inclined. Page 243." She picked up her book and tucked it under her arm.

I don't know what we would have done if Clarence hadn't come to the rescue. He kept away from Brian and me and went to the Brundages for TV as soon as he'd had his supper. He didn't come home till late. We thought he was sulking because of what we had done to him. And we didn't blame him. We'd been mean, and even when he'd helped us, our plan hadn't worked. But as things turned out, Clarence had done some thinking.

The next morning Clarence seemed to have turned over a new leaf. He did everything Aunt Minnie had been teaching him. Whenever she sat down, Clarence lay at her feet—in such a way she tripped over him as she got up. When Aunt Minnie walked, Clarence came smartly to heel—but so close that Aunt Minnie could hardly walk.

Clarence scoured the neighborhood and brought home a collection of old sticks and splintery bones. These he presented to Aunt Minnie.

Aunt Minnie had lectured Clarence on cleanliness. Now every time she took a bath, Clarence accompanied her and hung over the edge of the tub licking her legs.

He woke her at four every morning. Right on the hour, he would pad out of the kitchen, trot upstairs, and jump onto her bed. After running up and down the bed a few times, licking her face and biting her toes through the covers, Clarence would settle down to scratching himself. Then he would start running again. Finally, Aunt Minnie had to get up and let him out. Once out, Clarence disappeared just long enough to let Aunt Minnie get comfortably settled back in bed. Then he would bang on the door to get in.

After a few days, Aunt Minnie began to look rather pale and tired. She tried taking afternoon naps. Clarence joined her.

We didn't know what to do. It was all Aunt Minnie's fault that Clarence was being such a pest.

Aunt Minnie had spent an evening lecturing us on dog

care. "A dog should not be shut in the kitchen at night," she had read from page 475. "He must be allowed freedom in case of fire or attempted theft. Once a dog has been properly housebroken, there need be no concern about leaving him loose in the house. If he wishes to go out he will tell you."

With Aunt Minnie it is always easier to give in than to argue. There seemed no point in telling her what we had long ago discovered: Clarence is a friendly kind of dog who is likely to decide in the middle of the night that it would be pleasant to pay someone a visit.

Mother waited until Clarence had got Aunt Minnie up three times during one night. The next morning she said casually, "Clarence is just devoted to you, Aunt Minnie."

Aunt Minnie for once had nothing to say.

"I only wish," Mother went on, "that we could count on Jeffrey's getting on so well with Clarence. Jeffrey's coming very soon, you know."

Aunt Minnie thought a moment. She tried to move her feet and discovered Clarence was lying on them, quietly chewing the tip of her umbrella.

"I think," said Aunt Minnie, "that I must leave you soon. My cousin in Chicago has been expecting me for some time. And with Jeffrey coming you will need my room. No, no, don't urge me to stay. I really must be leaving."

She got up and went to pack, with Clarence at her heels.

"Brian!" she called a few minutes later. "Will you come and remove Clarence, please."

Brian came down carrying Clarence. He was trying to keep a straight face.

"What happened?" I asked.

"Clarence was freezing into position and being a show dog."

"So?"

"He was doing it right in Aunt Minnie's suitcase."

## 7. PET SHOW PROBLEM

"THERE now, I'm all packed." Aunt Minnie's train didn't leave till evening, but she believes in doing things in advance. She strolled over to the window and looked out. Brian and Clarence were sitting on the lawn.

"Wolf!" Brian called. "Wolf!"

Aunt Minnie's head jerked up. Her eyes brightened. Clutching her book in one hand she ran outside.

"Wolf! Wo—"

"Brian, stop that this minute!"

"Stop what, Aunt Minnie?"

Aunt Minnie opened her book. "This is really going too far, Brian. Surely even you must know the story of the boy who called 'Wolf!' He was a shepherd who amused himself by calling 'Wolf' and getting people to come help him when there was no wolf at all. And then one day . . . I'll find the story here in a minute and read it to you." She vigorously flipped over the pages of her book.

There was a great crashing in the bushes and a huge animal leaped toward them.

"Help! Wolf! Help! Help! Wolf!" cried Aunt Minnie. But she had courage. She stepped between Brian and the wolf.

The wolf stopped and looked at her. It panted, its huge jaws hanging open.

"Run, Brian! Run while you can," Aunt Minnie quavered. "Take Clarence with you." She continued to turn pages, probably looking for a section on how to deal with wolves.

"But it's just Wolf, Aunt Minnie."

"I know it's a wolf, Brian. I hope I can recognize one when I see it."

"Wolf won't hurt you. He's a friend of Clarence's."

"I don't care whose friend he is. Go in the house while you can."

Brian moved slowly toward the house, Clarence at his heels. "See you later, Wolf."

Aunt Minnie backed after him, never taking her eyes off the wolf. Safe inside, she said, "Just look a wild beast in the eye and it will not attack. Always remember that, Patricia."

"But that wasn't a wild beast, Aunt Minnie," I said. "That was George's dog. His *name* is Wolf."

Aunt Minnie sank into a chair and stared at us. "Well, I never."

"I was just calling him to practice tricks with Clarence for the pet show," Brian added.

"What pet show?" I asked.

Brian clapped a hand over his mouth. "I wasn't going

to tell you. It was going to be a surprise when we came home and Clarence had won a prize."

"When is it?"

"Tomorrow at school. You can enter any kind of pet and there are lots of prizes—for the most original pet, for the biggest and the smallest, for the prettiest and the funniest-looking. Clarence and Wolf are going to do tricks together and win a prize."

"Oh, good," I said, "we could hang the ribbon over his bed with his burglar medal."

"Don't count your chickens before they're hatched. Page 243," said Aunt Minnie recovering from her shock. "Clarence may not win and then you will be disappointed."

"He's got to win." Brian stood up. "I've told everybody how well he does tricks. I bet he's smarter than any other dog."

"He who laughs last laughs best," Aunt Minnie said, shaking her head. "Pride goeth before a fall," she added.

Clarence was trying to get a game of Fish started. There are two ways to play Fish. In the first, you throw Fish and Clarence brings it back. Then he puts it on the floor and stands back an inch or so. This gives you a fair chance to get Fish. If you get it before Clarence does, you may throw it again.

The other way to play Fish is more restful. Somebody covers Clarence's eyes while you hide Fish in the room. Clarence finds it by sniffing all over the room, for Fish smells strongly of vanilla. If Fish is well hidden there may be ten or fifteen minutes of peace before Clarence finds it.

Brian started to play with Clarence. Aunt Minnie was thumbing through her book. "Games," she muttered. "Here we are."

She turned to Brian and Clarence. "You are not playing that game correctly. I shall read you the rules."

"But there aren't any rules," Brian protested. "Clarence invented the game and we play by his rules."

"You see, Brian, you are contradicting yourself. In one breath you tell me there are no rules. And in the next you admit there are. Besides, I just put the rules into my book the other night."

Mother had been standing in the doorway. "There isn't time for a game anyway. I need Brian and Sis to help me with lunch."

"Only one more afternoon," Brian said between his teeth as we left the room. Clarence came with us, took one look at his neatly made bed, and lay down on the floor with a sigh.

It was right after dinner that night that the catastrophe happened. After dinner is the time when Clarence gets all ready to do his tricks. Usually he races into the living room before we've finished the dishes and is there waiting for us beside the box of dog candy. This evening he had insisted on going out. We could hear him barking furiously.

After a while I called him to come in. Clarence paid no attention and went on barking.

"I hope Clarence hasn't cornered a fierce wild beast," Brian said.

"There are no fierce wild beasts in this part of the country," Aunt Minnie said, consulting her book. "Why don't you take a flashlight and go out to see what it is?"

Brian stepped out the door and flashed his light into the bushes. "Oops!" he said in alarm. There was a moment of silence. "Ugh!" Brian cried.

Half a second later we understood what had happened. A horrible smell suddenly filled the room. One moment the room just smelled like itself and the next moment you couldn't smell a thing but skunk. My eyes watered and I could hardly bear to breathe.

Brian and Clarence burst into the house. Brian slammed the porch door behind them. "Clarence cornered a skunk," he explained.

"So I smell," Mother said grimly.

Aunt Minnie was trotting around the room fanning the air before her face with her book. "Oh dear," she said, "this is dreadful, dreadful."

Mother always stays calm in an emergency. She glanced quickly around the room, then pointed to the windows on the side away from the porch. "Sis, open those windows."

I threw them open. A fresh wave of skunk smell blew into the room. Before Mother could tell me to, I closed the windows.

"It's all around us. We're surrounded," Brian whispered hoarsely.

Aunt Minnie had stopped running. She was holding a handkerchief against her nose with one hand and flipping pages in her book with the other. "Of course," she said in a muffled voice. "The odor of skunk can be smelled for a radius of half a mile."

Mother happened to look at Clarence, who was running around the room with his head against the rug. "What is he doing?" she demanded.

"Trying to rub off some of the oil from the spray. The oil base gives the odor tremendous staying power," Aunt Minnie read with cheery interest.

"Put Clarence out!" Mother said.

"But—" I began.

"Sometimes," Aunt Minnie went on, "a heat wave occurring some six months after the incident will reactivate the odor."

Brian frowned slightly and looked at me.

"That means the heat starts the smell all over again," I said.

"Brian! Sis!" Mother commanded. "Put Clarence out this instant before he ruins the rug."

Brian and I closed in slowly on Clarence. I hadn't thought the smell could get any stronger, but the closer we came to Clarence the worse it was. Clarence flattened himself on the floor and rolled over on his back. He is very good at acting out "Don't beat me," even though no one ever has.

"Out, Clarence!"

Clarence crawled over the floor and lay down on Aunt Minnie's feet, the way she had taught him. He looked up appealingly at her.

"Well," said Aunt Minnie, "perhaps I could help you, Clarence."

"Could you, Aunt Minnie? Could you?" Brian asked.

She opened her book again and began to turn pages.

"Put Clarence out while Aunt Minnie is looking," Mother said.

"How can the house smell any worse?" I asked. "He's so unhappy! Let him stay."

"The skunk may still be there," Brian added.

Mother just looked at us.

We moved toward Clarence.

Seeing us approach, Clarence dashed across the floor, and jumped into Mother's lap for protection.

"Brian!"

I was surprised Mother didn't say more than that.

"Okay," he said, picking Clarence up.

"Love me, love my dog," I said, trying Aunt Minnie's method.

It didn't work. Clarence was put out. He huddled miserably against the door, trying to get back in.

Aunt Minnie was still turning pages. "I know there's something here on skunks." She turned page after page.

Clarence was pressing himself against the glass panes in the porch door. He looked very small and forlorn.

"Here we are," Aunt Minnie said finally. "Skunks." Everyone gave her full attention. "The skunk is found in all parts of North America, from Hudson Bay south to Mexico. There are several varieties of skunks. Some are spotted, some striped." We were squirming with impatience. "The skunk is a friendly, lazy animal which never attacks first. If endangered, the skunk will give warning by stamping its forefeet, then raising its tail. Skunks are fond of eating and should not be disturbed while so occupied. A skunk is the farmer's friend. It eats insects which destroy crops."

"What do you do after the skunk has attacked?" Mother asked, trying to hurry Aunt Minnie.

Clarence scratched pathetically at the door.

"It is not true that picking a skunk up by the tail will prevent it from attacking."

"But after the attack—what do you do?" Brian urged.

Aunt Minnie read on. "After the attack, you— Good heavens! My train! It's time to go."

"But you can't go yet!" I cried. "You've got to finish reading about skunks."

"Well," she said, "just for a minute. After the attack you, hmmm, you bury the offending object for several days and let the earth absorb its fumes."

"But Clarence isn't an offending object," I said.

"And we can't bury him," Brian added.

Aunt Minnie read on. "There is little that can be done to help a dog which has been attacked. Some recommend wrapping him in a burlap bag soaked with vinegar. This helps a little, but the owner should be warned that vinegar acts as a bleach. It will, for example, turn a brown dog pink."

Aunt Minnie snapped her book shut. "Now I really must go."

"Is that all your book says?" Brian asked. "Doesn't it tell how to unskunk a dog?"

Aunt Minnie was putting on her coat, straightening her hat, picking up her umbrella. "It seems to me there was something else, but I don't remember just where. If I find it I'll write to you. Well, children, good-by. Remember, it's always darkest before the dawn and every cloud has a silver lining."

Brian and I looked at each other.

"I'll let Clarence in while Mother's driving to the

station," he said. "She'll never know the difference the way the house smells."

Clarence crept in and lay down. He had no more bounce and gaiety. He looked as if he wanted to get rid of himself, but didn't know how.

"Well, Clarence," Brian said sadly, "you've really done it this time. How can I take a skunky dog to the pet show?"

Clarence wagged his tail a little.

"We could try vinegar," I suggested.

"I don't think I could take a pink-spotted dog either. Everybody would laugh."

We stared at each other in despair.

When Mother came home she said Clarence would have to sleep in the garage. "Aunt Minnie said the smell will wear off in about a week."

A whole week! I groaned and Brian rubbed at his eyes.

At seven the next morning, the phone rang. "I have a telegram for you," said a voice.

"Go ahead," I said.

"It reads: Just remembered pet show today. Found remedy. Sponge Clarence with tomato juice. All's well that ends well.

"It's signed Aunt Minnie."

I told Mother and Brian about the telegram. "It sounds pretty silly," I said, "but what can we lose?"

Brian and I cornered Clarence in the garage. Brian held him while I poured on tomato juice and rubbed it in.

After a couple of minutes, Brian said, "That's funny. I think the smell is gone."

"How can you tell? You smell, too, from handling Clarence."

"Let's ask Mother."

Mother assured us Clarence was unskunked. We popped him into a tub of warm water and washed him. Clarence came out fresh and clean and full of bounce. He seemed to have forgotten the skunk completely. We were still airing out corners of the house, but the worst was over.

It was late afternoon before Brian and Clarence came home from the pet show. I had been home from school for an hour and was waiting at the window.

"How did it go?"

"It was pretty good," Brian said. "Wolf won a prize as the biggest pet. George's family had come to take him and Wolf home. They were very pleased about the ribbon."

"Did Wolf and Clarence do tricks together?"

"No. Wolf did tricks, but Clarence wouldn't."

"What happened? Did you forget the dog candy, Brian?"

"No, I had it all right. Clarence just refused to do tricks."

I stared at Brian. "Clarence loves to do tricks. He's a big show-off."

Brian shrugged. "Billy Jones brought his pet skunk to the show."

"Oh," I said.

"Clarence took one look and climbed into my lap and wouldn't get down to do tricks. I guess he remembered all right. I guess he's learned his lesson."

"But that wasn't fair!" I looked hard at Brian and Clarence. They were looking awfully pleased with themselves, not at all the way anybody should look who had done badly and not even tried.

Brian reached into his pocket and slowly drew out a blue ribbon. Clarence ran circles around him and jumped into the air, trying to snatch the ribbon.

"Well, what *did* happen?" I asked. "Are you just telling me a story?"

"No, it's the truth."

"What did you get the ribbon for?"

"Best behaved pet in the show."

"*Clarence?*"

"Yup. When the judges came around and I put Clarence down, he heeled, and lay down, and then he stretched into show position. Just the way Aunt Minnie taught him."

## 8. A QUESTION OF HONESTY

"POOH," Brian said, "what a silly contest."

"What is?" I asked, looking up from my book.

"Why do you like cod liver oil?"

I stared past him at the rain-streaked window for a minute before I realized why I couldn't think of an answer. "I *don't* like cod liver oil."

"Nobody does. That's why it's so silly," Brian said. He brought over his magazine and showed me the contest. "All you have to do is complete this sentence in twenty-five words or less—I like Poindexter's Cod Liver Oil because . . ." He sighed. "How could anybody complete that sentence? You might say that you liked it *better* than other brands of cod liver oil because."

"Or," I said, "that you liked to give it to *somebody else* because." I took the magazine and studied the page.

"I don't suppose anybody will enter the contest," Brian went on.

"First prize a hundred dollars," I read.

"And all going to waste," Brian said sadly, "because nobody likes cod liver oil."

A brilliant idea came to me. "Brian," I said, "Clarence likes cod liver oil. When he was a puppy he just lapped it up. He could enter the contest."

"And win the hundred dollars!" Brian began dancing around the room.

Clarence, who had been sleeping quietly under the red chair, got up and joined in the dance. Then he came over and put his front paws and head in my lap. I showed him the magazine. "See, Clarence," I said, "all you have to do is say why you like cod liver oil and you'll win the prize. Won't that be fine?" Clarence's tail wagged.

Brian brought a piece of paper and a pencil from the desk and sat down near us. "I like," he wrote and stopped. Frowning, he asked, "Is it honest if Clarence has never taken *Poindexter's* Cod Liver Oil?"

"Of course," I said. "All cod liver oil tastes the same—awful. If you like one you like them all."

He looked at Clarence. "Why do you like cod liver oil?"

Clarence cocked his head and wagged his tail.

"He just likes it," I said.

Brian was impatient. "But he has to have a reason."

It took half an hour of hard work, but we finally got Clarence's reasons down on paper. "I like Poindexter's Cod Liver Oil because it tastes good and makes me feel good. It has given me strong bones, healthy teeth, lots of pep, and shiny fur."

"Twenty-two words," Brian said.

I peered over his shoulder. "I think we'd better say *hair*, not *fur*."

Brian looked puzzled. "But it's Clarence talking. It wouldn't be honest to say *hair* when we mean *fur.*"

"Well," I said, "I don't know how Mr. Poindexter will feel about a dog entering his contest."

"But Clarence isn't just a dog. He's one of the family. He's—he's a personality."

"We all know that," I pointed out, "but Mr. Poindexter doesn't. He hasn't met Clarence."

"Besides," Brian went on, "only somebody special like Clarence could truthfully say he liked cod liver oil."

I studied the paper again. "Perhaps we should take out the whole second sentence. Clarence himself doesn't know that cod liver oil has given him strong bones, healthy teeth, lots of pep, and shiny fur."

"We won't have much left."

"No," I admitted, "but it will all be true. Clarence does think it tastes good and anyone can tell it makes him feel good."

I wrote out the final version because my handwriting is better than Brian's. I signed it "Clarence Logan" because, as Brian said, Clarence is one of the family, so our family name must be his, too. As I was copying off the address, I happened to notice rule 5. "Oops, we have to send a label from a bottle of Poindexter's Cod Liver Oil."

Brian looked at the weather and made a face. "I guess I could go down on my bike and get a bottle. I'll take the letter along and mail it as soon as I get the label."

When Brian returned he was carrying one of the largest bottles of cod liver oil I had ever seen. "What did you buy, the large economy size?"

"This was the only size they had," he explained. "I

didn't have enough money to pay for it, so I charged it to Mother. I imagine she'll be glad we spent her money on something worth while for once."

"I thought it would be nice to keep the contest a secret and surprise Mother when Clarence wins."

"Let's!" Brian agreed enthusiastically.

"We can't, though, if the bill from the drugstore comes on the first of next month. The contest results won't be announced until the seventh."

Brian considered the problem. "We could let Clarence open the bill. They'll send another the next month."

Clarence is very good about carrying in letters from the mailbox, except that he likes to open them himself. And when Clarence opens the mail, nobody can make head or tail out of the shreds he spits out.

"What shall we spend the prize for? I know," Brian rushed on, "let's get a ping-pong table for us and a fur coat for Mother."

"Wait a minute," I said. "The hundred dollars won't be ours. Clarence is the one who entered the contest. We just did the writing for him."

"I biked into town in the rain."

"I don't care," I said. "It's Clarence's money. But he isn't selfish. He'd be willing to buy something everyone can enjoy."

"I bet Clarence would give me half. Wouldn't you, Clarence?"

Clarence leaped into Brian's lap and licked his face.

"He probably would," I said, "but I'm not going to let him. He'll spend the money himself. I imagine he wants a television set. We could get one secondhand."

Brian liked that idea all right, and Clarence seemed so pleased we thought he must have understood what we were saying.

When you're waiting for something good, like Christmas or a prize in a contest, time just creeps by. Brian and I had never lived through such a long month. Only Clarence didn't mind. He was even busier than usual because a man came to paint the shutters. Clarence had to supervise the man, then help him eat his lunch. At night, though he was tired, Clarence lay first on my bed, then on Brian's, and last on Mother's, giving each of us a turn so no one's feelings would be hurt.

On the twenty-eighth of the month, the first problem arose. The drugstore sent its bill ahead of time. Brian and I hadn't started watching for it so soon, and Mother got it.

She opened the envelope, glanced at the bill, and started to lay it on the desk. Then she picked it up again. "They've made a mistake," she said. "I haven't bought any cod liver oil."

Brian and I looked at each other. We hadn't thought of what we were going to say if this happened.

Brian took a deep breath. "I bought it," he said.

"*You* bought a bottle of cod liver oil?" Mother could hardly believe her ears.

"Yes," Brian said, recklessly quoting an advertisement he had heard on the radio. "I was feeling nervous and run-down, so I bought a bottle. I didn't think you'd mind."

Of all the unlikely stories he could have invented, this was the worst.

Mother sat down. Then she pulled herself together and said, "Let me see the bottle."

There is simply no point in trying to lie to Mother, even if it's in a good cause. With an unhappy glance at me, Brian went to find the bottle.

Mother took it and examined it. "Just the sight of the bottle cured you, I see." It hadn't been opened. "The label is gone. Well, you know the rule, Brian."

The rule was that we could buy something like cereal if we wanted box tops, but we had to eat what we'd bought.

Brian turned pale.

Mother handed him the bottle. "Put it near your place in the dining room," she said cheerfully.

"Couldn't I keep it in the kitchen for Clarence?" Brian asked.

"No, Clarence doesn't need cod liver oil in summer."

"What about me?" Brian cried. "I don't need it in summer either."

"But you're nervous and run-down," Mother said. "It will be just the thing for you. I'm glad you got a large bottle."

As she left the room, I could see she was smiling, so I knew she was just teaching Brian a lesson. She wasn't really going to make him take the whole bottle. That was a relief. Otherwise, to be fair, I'd have had to take half the bottle.

"You should have told the truth—that we needed the label," I said.

"I know. But I thought she might ask what kind of contest we needed the label for. And I didn't want to tell

Clarence's secret. I hope she breaks down after a day or two."

Mother did, of course, but by then Brian had a new worry. "It was awful stuff," he told me when Mother had thrown out the bottle. "The worst I'd ever tasted. I don't think even Clarence could like it."

"Don't say that! If he doesn't like it, he can't accept the prize. It wouldn't be honest."

"Too late to find out now," Brian said so cheerfully that I wondered if he had deliberately delayed telling me this.

The second problem arose just a few days later. One morning there was an envelope in the mail addressed to Mr. Clarence Logan. "It's come! It's come!" Brian shouted. Instead of tearing it open right then and there, we let Clarence carry it into the house because, after all, it was his letter. He pranced across the lawn ahead of us. As soon as we got in, Brian snatched the letter from Clarence and started to open it.

"Stop!" I cried. "He's my dog. Let me open it."

"I took the cod liver oil," Brian said grimly. "I'm going to open the letter." He drew it out and shook the envelope. There was no check.

"Read what it says," I urged.

"Dear Mr. Logan," Brian read. "That's you, Clarence."

Encouraged by this, Clarence bounded into the air and grabbed the letter. I made a dive for him, but he thought it was a game, banged open the screen door, and dashed outside. By the time we caught up with him, the letter had been chewed into small, soggy pieces. Clarence lay under a bush, panting and wagging his tail. It had been a fine game and he had won.

"Clarence—" Brian began in a threatening tone.

I interrupted. "It *was* his letter, Brian. Besides, you can't bring it back."

Brian sighed. "Wonder what it said."

The only thing to do, we decided, was wait. Probably the letter had been congratulating Clarence and telling him that the prize check would arrive in a few days. We would wait a week. Then if we hadn't had further news, we could write and explain that the letter had been lost.

Four days of the week had gone by when Mother came to find Clarence, Brian, and me in the garden. There was an odd look on her face as she said, "There is a gentleman here to see Mr. Clarence Logan."

The bottom of my stomach dropped away as if I were on an elevator.

In a small voice Brian suggested, "Couldn't you say Clarence is out just now and you don't know when he'll be back?"

"I am not going to lie, Brian," Mother said, "and the gentleman says he has an appointment. He wrote to Mr. Clarence Logan saying he would like to come this afternoon and asking Mr. Clarence Logan to telephone him if this date was not convenient."

"Oh," Brian said.

I couldn't tell whether Mother was angry or amused, but she didn't seem inclined to help us. "I suggest you go in and see the gentleman," she said.

As soon as Mother was out of earshot, Brian whispered, "Sis, what are we going to do? I thought they'd just send the prize. How could I know they were going to send someone to see Clarence?"

I looked at Clarence, who was lying in a patch of sunshine gently wagging his tail. "It won't be fair," I said, "if they take the prize back because Clarence is a dog. Clarence gave an honest answer and he deserves to win. Poor Clarence!" I said. "Brian, suppose there's some law we don't know about that says dogs can't enter contests. It would be terrible if he got into trouble."

Clarence climbed into my lap.

"Sis, I know! Why can't I pretend to be Clarence? I'll be glad to do it." Brian got up.

"Would that be honest?"

"Just as honest as it would be for them to take back the prize because Clarence is a dog. His answer won and I'm just seeing to it that he gets the prize. Come on!"

I got up and followed Brian. I still wasn't convinced, but I didn't want Clarence to get in trouble or be laughed at. He can't bear being laughed at.

"Let's leave Clarence outside," Brian said as we reached the door. "We don't want to make a mistake and call him by name."

Clarence didn't like being left out. He banged noisily on the porch door. We paid no attention.

A stout, elderly gentleman stood up and pumped Brian's hand vigorously. "Well, well, young sir. I had expected someone older."

"I'm ten," Brian said, a little annoyed.

"Are you Mr. Poindexter?" I asked.

"No, no, young lady. My name is Cole. I am Mr. Poindexter's representative."

We all sat down. Brian and I looked uneasily at Mr. Cole. He had a ruddy, pleasant face, the kind of face that usually belongs to people who like animals and children. But, of course, he was Mr. Poindexter's representative, and there was no telling how Mr. Poindexter felt about children and animals.

Mr. Cole unlocked a big, brown, leather brief case. It wasn't the kind of brief case Brian and I have for school, with a flap. This one balanced on a flat bottom and pulled open at the top. Mr. Cole removed some papers and began to go through them.

"Yes, yes," he said, "here we are. A very fine statement, young sir. The judges were well impressed with its simpleness and sincerity. My congratulations."

Mother must have let Clarence in through the kitchen, for just at that moment he came bounding across the room. He was so pleased to be in and find we had company that he raced round and round the room, jumped from my lap into Brian's, and then into Mr. Cole's.

"Cl— ah, get down!" I ordered.

Clarence didn't realize I was talking to him. He gently nipped Mr. Cole's nose.

"Down!" I repeated.

Clarence lay down in Mr. Cole's lap and looked innocently at me. He began to chew on the papers Mr. Cole was holding.

"Careful," Brian said, lifting Clarence down. "That's what happened to the letter you wrote us," he explained to Mr. Cole. "Cl—that is, the dog chewed it up and so we didn't know you were coming."

"Fine dog, fine dog," Mr. Cole said. "What's his name?"

"Brian," Brian said.

"Here, Brian," Mr. Cole snapped his fingers.

Clarence was puzzled. He heard the tone of voice people use when they're calling him, but he also knew who Brian was. Clarence knew *he* wasn't called Brian. He looked at the real Brian.

Brian smiled weakly. "Go on," he urged.

"Well, now, Clarence," Mr. Cole began, "our company—"

At the sound of his name Clarence went over and licked Mr. Cole's hand.

"—our company would like you and your mother to give us permission to use your prize-winning statement in advertisements, perhaps with your photo. What do you say to that, Clarence?"

Clarence, pleased with all this talk about himself, jumped back into Mr. Cole's lap and started to chew on the papers again.

"Down, Brian!" I said.

Clarence paid no attention. I lifted him off. He began to untie Mr. Cole's shoelaces.

"Now, now, young lady," Mr. Cole said, "leave Brian alone. He isn't doing any harm. What a fine, healthy dog he is, full of spirit and fun. He would make a magnificent advertisement for our company. But I guess you haven't sampled Poindexter's Cod Liver Oil, have you, Brian?"

The real Brian and I exchanged heartsick glances. If only we had let Clarence handle his own affairs!

"Of course, Clarence," said Mr. Cole addressing Brian, "we should like to make sure of the truthfulness of your statement. I myself can tell by your face that you're an honest boy. But Mr. Poindexter wishes to make sure that if someone says he likes Poindexter's Cod Liver Oil he

POINDEXTER'S
COD LIVER
OIL

really likes it. You were the only winner who came right out and said you yourself liked it, you know."

"Were there other contestants?" I asked in surprise.

"Indeed yes, indeed yes. Hundreds. But most of them said they liked our product because it was good for their children, or words to that effect."

Mr. Cole reached into his brief case and produced a large bottle of Poindexter's Cod Liver Oil. He filled a small paper cup and handed it to Brian. "Just try that, Clarence."

Brian wet his lips, took a deep breath, and downed the cod liver oil. For a second I thought everything was going to be all right. Then Brian shuddered. "Ugh!" he exclaimed.

A look of sorrow came over Mr. Cole's pleasant face. He put the top back on his bottle and placed the bottle in his brief case.

The real Clarence began nosing about in the brief case. "Stop it, Brian," I cried loudly and angrily.

That brought Mother into the room. "Brian, what are you doing?" Then she saw Clarence. The front half of him had disappeared into Mr. Cole's brief case. All that could be seen of Clarence were his hind legs kicking wildly in the air and his tail, which was wagging. "Clarence!" Mother pulled him out of the brief case. "You're a bad dog, Clarence!"

Clarence put his tail between his legs and hid behind Mr. Cole's feet.

Mr. Cole looked at each of us. His face grew even sadder. "Do I understand that the dog's name is Clarence and yours is Brian?" he asked Brian.

Mother answered. "If these children have told you anything else, Mr. Cole, I must apologize. I thought I had brought them up to be honest." She sounded very angry.

"But we were honest," I wailed. "That was the whole trouble."

"You see," Brian said earnestly, "I hate cod liver oil. So does Sis. I think Mother does, too."

Mr. Cole nodded dismally.

"But," I went on, "Clarence always used to love cod liver oil. We thought you had to tell the truth in the contest."

"So Clarence was the only one who could enter," Brian finished. "He gave only true reasons and they were the kind of reasons—"

Mr. Cole looked at Clarence's letter. "Yes, yes. Your handwriting, but I can see these are Clarence's reasons."

"We thought you'd just send him the hundred-dollar prize," Brian went on. "When you came to see Clarence we were afraid you would take back the prize if you discovered he was a dog."

"I see the whole thing," Mr. Cole said. "But—does the real Clarence like Poindexter's Cod Liver Oil?"

"I'll get a saucer." Brian dashed out of the room.

I hoped it would be all right. I thought the cod liver oil was what Clarence had been looking for in Mr. Cole's bag. But I wasn't sure. It would be awful if he didn't like it. Clarence is a fussy eater and when he doesn't like something he as good as says, "This is disgusting." He shudders and backs slowly away from it, lifting his paws like a cat walking in wet grass.

Mr. Cole brought out his bottle and poured a large portion of cod liver oil into the saucer. He placed the saucer on the floor.

Clarence came out from his hiding place and sniffed cautiously. He advanced a little and sniffed again. He drew back. I held my breath. Clarence advanced. He tried a little, then licked up every drop, polished the saucer, and looked hopefully at the bottle.

A broad smile spread across Mr. Cole's face. "Well done, Clarence, well done," he said. "We shall be glad to have you on our list of winners."

We had a nice visit with Mr. Cole while Mother signed papers allowing Clarence's statement to be used. We told Mr. Cole he could get a good picture of Clarence at the newspaper office, and then we told him about Clarence's catching a burglar. Clarence brought Fish and played with Mr. Cole.

Finally Mr. Cole stood up to leave.

"About the prize," I said. "Could you send cash instead of a check? I don't know whether the bank will let Clarence cash a check."

"Check? What check?" Mr. Cole asked.

"The hundred dollars," Brian explained.

Mr. Cole smiled. "I'm afraid Clarence didn't win first prize. He's getting a special prize for sincerity, and it isn't money. But don't worry, he'll like it just as well."

Later, after Mother had heard the story again, she said, "Well, I hope you've learned a lesson. Clarence gave an honest answer and won a prize. He almost lost his prize because Brian, aided by Sis, was dishonest. But when Mr. Cole heard the truth and met the real Clarence everything was fine again."

Brian and I had thought all along, of course, that honesty was the best policy. Our mistake had been in not trusting Clarence and Mr. Poindexter. So when the prize came we thought it only honest and right to let Clarence keep the whole thing. He is a generous dog and would have been glad to share with us, but we felt the prize belonged to him alone.

The prize was a case of Poindexter's Cod Liver Oil.

## 9. ADVENTURES IN HUNTING

In a way, it was all because of the early fall of snow that Uncle Jeffrey decided to turn Clarence into a hunting dog. Two things happened.

First, because of the snow, Uncle Jeffrey was taking his exercise on our porch. He was marching up and down, like a sentry on duty, doing "left face" and "right face" and "about face." Brian and Clarence were marching behind him, doing whatever Uncle Jeffrey did. That is, Brian was imitating Uncle Jeffrey. Clarence isn't very good at doing "right face" because it's difficult with four feet.

A rabbit came bounding across the snow. Clarence dashed out to meet it, tail wagging, ready to touch noses and make friends. The rabbit took one look at Clarence and fled. Clarence was disappointed. Then he started running, bouncing into the air the way he had seen the rabbit do.

Uncle Jeffrey was shocked. "Look at that!" he said.

"Tried to make friends with the rabbit. Now he's imitating the rabbit. What way is that for a dog to act?"

Uncle Jeffrey stood frowning, trying to think of some way to make Clarence more like other dogs.

The second thing happened after Uncle Jeffrey cleaned his hunting gun. He decided to try a few shots just for fun. He took his gun and went just outside the house. Clarence and Brian and I went, too. Uncle Jeffrey aimed into the air and fired.

Brian jumped. Clarence put his tail between his legs and fled.

"Disgraceful!" Uncle Jeffrey shouted.

He never had a chance to say just what was disgraceful. The gun's explosion had loosened a heavy layer of wet snow on the sloping roof. With a crash it slid off.

Uncle Jeffrey vanished from sight. One minute he was standing there as big as life. The next minute he was gone. All we could see was a big lump under the snow. I guess Uncle Jeffrey had had the breath knocked out of him, for he didn't even stir.

Fortunately, Brian and Clarence knew just what to do. They had seen a television program about monks and St. Bernards looking for travelers lost in the snowy Alps.

Brian ran and brought a pointed stick. Clarence dashed around in circles sniffing the snow while Brian poked with his stick. To make the hunt more exciting, they pretended they weren't sure where Uncle Jeffrey was buried.

Finally Brian began poking the lump that was Uncle Jeffrey. "Here, Clarence," he called. "There's something here!" Clarence was already digging hard where Uncle

Jeffrey's head was. The snow flew up in a shower from his feet.

Uncle Jeffrey got up, brushing the snow from his clothing. He swung his arms in circles and moved his head stiffly. Then he stamped off into the house without even saying "Thank you" to his rescuers.

Brian said, "Is he angry because we rescued him?"

"I think Uncle Jeffrey would rather rescue other people than be rescued," I told him.

That evening Uncle Jeffrey found a way to get the upper hand again. "You know what I'm going to do?" he asked in the tone of a person who is going to do you a big favor. "I'm going to take Clarence hunting. Make a real dog out of him."

"But Clarence *is* a real dog, Uncle Jeffrey," Brian protested.

"I'll take you, too," Uncle Jeffrey went on. "Lots of things you can learn."

"Oh, boy," Brian said, "I'll take my bee-bee gun and hunt squirrels."

"You will not," Uncle Jeffrey said. "Neither you nor Clarence knows anything about hunting and you are going to watch and learn. I shall borrow a setter, a real hunting dog. Clarence will watch the setter and learn how to behave in the field. You will watch me. If you're good you may carry the game bag," he added. "Furthermore, we are not going after squirrels. We are hunting pheasant."

"When are you going on the hunt?" I asked.

"As soon as the snow is gone." Uncle Jeffrey got up to go to bed. He was limping slightly from being poked with

Brian's stick and his face was scratched from being unburied by Clarence.

"The hunt doesn't sound like much fun," I commented. "I'm glad Uncle Jeffrey isn't teaching me to hunt."

"Clarence will show him," Brian said. "Clarence is a better, smarter dog than any old setter."

The hunt got off two mornings later. Uncle Jeffrey had borrowed a big red Irish setter. It was a beautiful dog and so well trained it did everything Uncle Jeffrey told it to. Clarence tried to play with the setter. He jumped up and bit its ears. The setter paid no attention. It just waited for Uncle Jeffrey's next command.

The hunting party assembled outside the house. Brian was carrying the game bag and the lunch. Uncle Jeffrey was carrying the gun. Mother came rushing out and handed Uncle Jeffrey a small package of crackers. "For Clarence," she explained. "He's accustomed to a snack at eleven."

"Bah," said Uncle Jeffrey. "Ridiculous. Be too busy hunting to stop for crackers. Do Clarence good to wait for his one big meal." But he stuffed the crackers into his pocket anyway.

Then Clarence decided to take Fish. Somebody might feel like a game later.

Halfway down the road Uncle Jeffrey noticed Clarence had brought Fish. He snatched Fish away and put it in his pocket. Probably it wasn't dignified for a hunting dog to be carrying a rubber fish.

As they disappeared around a bend, Uncle Jeffrey was striding ahead, Brian trotting behind, and Clarence jumping on the setter, trying to play. The setter just followed Uncle Jeffrey.

Clarence was the first one home from the hunt. He arrived at noon and crawled wearily into bed. Mother was so sorry for him that she scrambled an egg just for Clarence. After he had eaten, he went to sleep.

Brian was the next one home. He arrived at three in the afternoon. "Is Clarence here?" he asked anxiously.

"Sound asleep," I told him. "Why are the two of you home? Is the hunt over?"

"No." Brian pulled off his wet shoes. Clarence padded in and joined him. "Clarence didn't enjoy the hunt. He kept chasing squirrels and barking and digging in the leaves and disturbing the setter. Uncle Jeffrey kept yelling at him. And Uncle Jeffrey wouldn't stop for an eleven o'clock snack. Finally Clarence sneaked away and disappeared. Uncle Jeffrey wouldn't let me call him. He said we'd do better without Clarence. I was afraid Clarence would get lost."

"So then what happened?"

"Then we went on hunting. But Uncle Jeffrey takes such big steps. And the game bag was heavy. And he wouldn't stop for lunch."

"Didn't you have any lunch?" Mother asked.

"Finally," Brian said. "After I asked for the third time, Uncle Jeffrey took the game bag and left me on a log to have lunch. He said he'd come back later and get me. But he didn't."

"What!" said Mother.

"I ate my lunch. And then I waited and waited. Uncle

DOG
BISCUITS

Jeffrey didn't come. By then I was hungry again, so I thought probably he didn't want his lunch anyway and I ate it. He still didn't come. After a while I came home."

"I hope nothing's happened to Jeffrey," Mother said more or less to herself. "This isn't like him at all." She looked at her watch. "Well, we'll give him a little more time."

At five o'clock there was no sign of Uncle Jeffrey.

At six it was dark. Uncle Jeffrey still wasn't home.

At seven we had supper. Mother was beginning to talk about calling the police.

"Uncle Jeffrey won't like it if we send the police after him and he isn't really lost," Brian said.

By eight we were really beginning to worry.

"Maybe he *is* lost," I said.

Clarence brought Bone and started to play with me.

"Maybe Clarence could find him," Brian suggested.

"Where's Uncle Jeffrey?" I asked Clarence. "Find Uncle Jeffrey."

Clarence looked around and then brought Ball.

"Not Ball, Clarence. Find Uncle Jeffrey." Clarence wagged his tail.

Brian had an idea. "Find Fish, Clarence."

Clarence sniffed all over the room, looking for Fish. Fish wasn't there. He sat down to think where he had left Fish. We could almost see the thoughts going through his head. Where was Fish? Uncle Jeffrey had Fish. Uncle Jeffrey wasn't here. Fish was lost, too. Clarence whimpered. The crease in his forehead deepened.

"Find Fish," Brian said again.

Clarence thought some more. If he could find Uncle

Jeffrey, he would find Fish. He decided to look for Uncle Jeffrey.

The three of us took flashlights and followed Clarence, who was running ahead, nose to the ground. He led us deep into the woods. After half an hour we found Uncle Jeffrey. He was sitting on a log eating Clarence's crackers. Clarence sniffed him all over.

"Ah, there you are," Uncle Jeffrey said, as if *he* had found *us*.

We all started for home.

"Were you lost, Uncle Jeffrey?" Brian asked, when we were finally seated round the fire.

"Certainly not," he said. "Well," he added as we looked at him, "of course I don't know these woods very well. I may have lost my bearings a little when the sun went down. But I could have found my way back in the morning." Then the whole story came out.

"Was disappointed in Clarence and Brian," Uncle Jeffrey said. "Neither of them seemed to catch on. When Clarence left, I thought things would go better. Then Brian wanted to interrupt the hunt for lunch. Left him, meaning to come back.

"Followed the setter deep into the woods and found some excellent game. Dog was working well and it seemed a shame to go back before we finished that particular area.

"Suddenly realized it was later than I had thought. No point in going back for Brian. Surely he would have gone home."

"I might still be sitting there!" Brian whispered to me.

"We went deeper into the woods. By this time darkness

was falling. Not completely sure where I was. Thought the best thing would be to follow the setter home. So I said, 'Home!' to him."

"Then what happened?" I asked.

"Dog bolted into the bushes and went home. Left me there holding the game bag."

Uncle Jeffrey paused and stared at the fire.

I wanted to say, "What about Clarence? Didn't he find you? Shouldn't he be praised?" But I didn't dare. Perhaps Uncle Jeffrey didn't like to admit Clarence had found him.

Just then Uncle Jeffrey spoke again. "You know," he said, "I misjudged Clarence's talents. Mistake to think he ought to be a hunting dog. Actually is a tracking dog, and a very fine one. Probably got a bit of bloodhound in him. You ought to train him more. Not many dogs can track so well."

I was very pleased with this fine compliment. "Do you still have Fish in your pocket?" I was pretty sure he did. Clarence had been nosing and pawing the pocket ever since we got home.

Uncle Jeffrey pulled out Fish. "Blasted nuisance," he said. Clarence snatched Fish and took it away to a safe place in the kitchen.

We didn't tell Uncle Jeffrey it was Fish that Clarence had been looking for. Uncle Jeffrey was pleased to believe Clarence had been looking for him.

"How about going tracking next week?" he asked Brian. "We won't take the setter. Just you and me and Clarence."

"Oh, boy," Brian said.

Uncle Jeffrey got up. "Think I'll take a hot bath, then have something to eat." He handed Mother the bag of pheasants. "One of these is for Clarence. After you've roasted it, cut it up into small pieces for him. Mind he doesn't get any bones. And don't give him the whole bird at one meal. He's too small.

"But very intelligent," he added.

We had known that all along. So had Clarence.

## 10. DISCOVERY OF A SECRET

CLARENCE had a secret, and he wasn't letting any of us in on it. Usually in the morning he dashes out and comes right back in again to claim part of my breakfast. Clarence is very fond of bacon and eggs, but he seldom gets any all to himself.

Now, as soon as Mother let him out, he raced away at top speed and didn't come back for breakfast. Mostly, he didn't come back until noon. Then he would go away for the afternoon, still looking very secret-y and important.

Clarence even gave up going to see television. The Brundages called to ask if he were sick. We explained that he was just busy.

Brian and I tried following him. But Clarence runs much faster than we do, and all we'd see would be his long, curly tail disappearing into the bushes.

So we tried pretending we didn't care what his secret was. That didn't work either. He just went trotting smartly off to wherever it was he went.

Right in the middle of the mystery, Brian was invited to visit Uncle Peter in New York during Thanksgiving vacation. At least, we thought it was Brian who was invited.

Just to show you what Uncle Peter's like, when he came to visit us he wanted to know where we'd got Clarence. He had forgotten that he sent me Clarence. Then he wanted to know why we called the dog Clarence. Of course, it was Uncle Peter who had named him. Then Uncle Peter remembered what had happened. He had meant to call the dog Spot. But he had been writing that same day to a business friend whose name is Clarence. And he got mixed up. You would never guess that Uncle Peter is a successful businessman, the way he keeps forgetting everyday things.

Anyway, when the invitation came from Uncle Peter Mother could hardly believe her eyes.

"I am very much taken with that young chap of yours, Clarence," Uncle Peter wrote. "And I should like to have him visit me in New York for a few days. Naturally, I would take the best care of him. He can sleep on the couch in my living room. We'll eat in the best restaurants, visit the zoo, go to the park, go up in the Empire State Building. I think you'll agree with me that Clarence is the kind of young fellow who would benefit from such a trip."

"He can't mean that," Mother said.

"I bet Uncle Peter really means he wants me to come for a visit," Brian said. "Doesn't he, Mother?"

I didn't agree. "Maybe he does mean Clarence. Clarence would love to go to the zoo and eat in the best restaurants."

"Don't be silly," Brian said. "Of course he means me. He's just mixed up the names."

"Well, if he's mixed up the names, perhaps he means *me,* not you. How do you know?"

"Because Uncle Peter says 'he' not 'her.' "

"Suppose he's mixed that up, too?"

"Oh, he means me," said Brian. "Doesn't he, Mother?"

"Perhaps," she said, still studying the letter.

"What's more," I said, "Clarence is my dog. So if the invitation is addressed to Clarence and he doesn't go, I ought to be the one to go."

"Uncle Peter means *me,*" Brian insisted.

Brian worked on Mother some more and finally she agreed that he must be the one Uncle Peter was inviting. She wrote accepting the invitation.

"Clarence can't go anyway," Brian said, ignoring me, "because he's too busy. If Uncle Peter calls me Clarence, should I answer to that?"

"No, you can tell him your own name," Mother said.

So off Brian went.

I was sulking. I thought Mother might at least have written to ask whether Uncle Peter wanted Brian or me, or even both of us. Brian had no right to grab the trip. And I was deserted even by Clarence, who was too busy with his own affairs to stay home and play.

When he was home, he was bossy. He ran everything and everyone. He slept on our beds. He insisted on carrying part of the mail and then opening it. He showed all the tradesmen the way into the house, going back to worry their trouserlegs if they paused on the way. He supervised my bath. He inspected the house after it had been cleaned. He opened doors that had been closed, and closed doors that had been open. If we had company, Clarence took over and entertained all evening with tricks and games and songs.

The last straw came at dinner one night. Mother went into the kitchen just as I went to the telephone. When I came back into the dining room, there was Clarence, sitting in my chair eating my cake. Instead of jumping down and looking ashamed, he just glanced at me and went on eating.

I didn't say anything, as I got another plate and another piece of cake and another chair. But I thought, "All right, Clarence. Enough's enough. I'm going to find out what this secret is that's making you so important."

I had to use trickery. First I collected a batch of tiny pebbles. Then I painted them red. I sewed a little bag with a hole at the bottom, just big enough for the pebbles to fall through if the bag was shaken. I filled the bag and attached it to Clarence's collar first thing in the morning before he went out. He didn't like this at all, but he was in such a hurry to be off that he didn't try to get rid of the bag.

After breakfast I went outside to pick up the trail. It wasn't easy, because the pebbles were scattered pretty far apart. But I managed. Eventually I arrived at a barn.

I stood, looking around and seeing nothing unusual. Clarence came trotting out of the barn and I stepped quickly around the corner. He didn't see me and went off toward home.

Into the barn I went. Again I saw nothing unusual. But after poking around a little I heard a faint noise and went toward it. Bedded down in straw in an old stall, I found seven puppies and their mother. Then I understood. Clarence had been spending his time visiting here. He just loves puppies.

So do I. I was still admiring the pups when Mrs. Olsen arrived with their breakfast.

"Why, hello, Sis," she said. "How did you get here?"

"I followed Clarence," I admitted.

"He's very devoted—spends practically all day over here. I don't know what he's going to do when I move the family into the cellar tomorrow. But it's getting too chilly out here." She busied herself putting down the pan. The pups tumbled over one another in their eagerness to get the milk.

"They're awful cute," I said. "Three of them look just like your Bonnie."

"Yes, they're already promised, but I don't know what we're going to do with the other four. Would you like them?"

"Oh, I'd love them." I was all set to take them home. Then a thought struck me. "But I'd better ask Mother first."

"All right."

"Could I tell you tomorrow? Would that be too late? Would you have given them away by then?"

"Goodness, no," she laughed. "They can't leave their

mother for several weeks yet. By Christmas they should be ready. Take your time. There's no rush."

I went home in a daze. Think of it—four puppies. Wouldn't Clarence be pleased! And Brian, too.

Mother was in the kitchen. "I have the most wonderful chance," I said.

"Really, dear?"

"Mrs. Olsen's going to give me four puppies."

"What?" Mother said.

"Mrs. Olsen's going to give me four puppies," I repeated patiently.

Mother turned to face me. "Four puppies? Sis, we can't take all those puppies. That's too many. And Clarence's feelings would be hurt."

"No, they wouldn't. He loves puppies. That's where he's been—visiting them. And four isn't really too many. We've got lots of room."

"I'm sorry," she said firmly, "but we are not taking four puppies."

"Three?"

"No."

"Two?"

"No."

"One?"

"No."

"Not even one tiny puppy to be company for Clarence?"

"No."

"Not even one?"

Mother sighed. "We'll see."

That was a good sign. It meant she was weakening. If

I kept up my campaign and Brian helped, she would surely give in on one puppy and maybe even two by Christmas. And if you're going to have two puppies you might just as well have three or four.

I couldn't wait to get Brian alone that evening when he came back from Uncle Peter's. But it took time. Mother wanted to hear all about his trip. Brian talked a lot, yet you could see he was holding something back.

He didn't tell what it was until Clarence came in, jumped all over him, and organized two games at once—one with me and one with Brian.

Then Brian said to all three of us, "Uncle Peter wasn't mixed up at all this time."

Nobody said anything.

"It really was Clarence he was inviting."

Mother said, "Brian, don't be silly. If Peter said that, he was only teasing you. Nobody would invite a dog to New York to go sight-seeing."

"Uncle Peter would." Brian was quite serious. "He said he thought travel would be broadening for Clarence. And he said he enjoyed Clarence's company. I'm sorry I took your trip, Clarence."

Mother studied Brian's face a minute and decided there wasn't any joke. She reached out and ruffled his hair. "Was it all right when Peter discovered Clarence hadn't come?"

"Oh, yes." Brian sounded more cheerful. "Once he found there was only me, he said it didn't really matter because he could take me all the places he'd planned to take Clarence. If it had been the other way round it might have been more difficult. I mean, Clarence couldn't have gone to some of the places Uncle Peter might have planned for me. And he said maybe Sis and Clarence could visit him after Christmas."

I began to feel very friendly toward Brian again. As soon as we were alone, I said, "I found out where Clarence was going."

"Where?"

"To visit some puppies over there." I waved my hand vaguely. Then before he could ask me where the puppies were, I told him about my plan and we began to figure out ways to persuade Mother.

Brian suggested, "After Christmas would be a good time. With company coming and all the things to do, she won't feel much like puppies before Christmas. Where are the puppies? Can I see them?"

"Maybe I could take you some time. The lady that owns them has put them in her cellar now." I was counting on Christmas to put them out of his mind.

If Brian knew they were at the Olsens', he'd go right over. I was feeling a little mean about having tricked Clarence. So I thought at least I could keep part of his secret until he wanted us to know. If Brian saw the four puppies that didn't look like Bonnie, he would know the secret right away, just as I had.

Clarence was a father.

## 11. CHRISTMAS SURPRISE

IT was almost Christmas, and Christmas is the holiday Clarence enjoys most. He doesn't know what it's really about, of course. All Clarence knows is that Christmas is a time when there are lots of packages. And packages mean paper to tear and balls of string to unwind.

Once Clarence thought we were having Christmas in August. That was when the United Parcels man made a delivery at our house. It was a hot day and Mother offered the man a cold ginger ale. While the man was drinking it, Clarence got into his truck, unrolled four balls of string and untied a few parcels. Brian said the man should change his sign from United Parcels to Untied Parcels. But the man was nice about it, though he never parks near our house any more.

To get back to Christmas, it looked as if this would be a fine one. Uncle Jeffrey was coming. So was Aunt Minnie. And maybe even Uncle Peter. There was an extra big pile of presents under the tree.

The only one of us who wasn't excited was Clarence. For some reason he seemed a little sad. When we were tying up some last-minute presents, Clarence just sat and watched. He didn't try to take away the ribbon or get his paws into the packages the way he usually does. Perhaps, I thought, he was missing the puppies. He had been staying home lately. But then, he had been staying home for several weeks.

"Perhaps he's sick," I said.

"No," Brian said. "Clarence told me it was because he hadn't got his allowance and he hasn't any presents for anyone."

"Brian, Clarence doesn't ever get an allowance."

"That's the trouble."

"And besides, he doesn't know about giving presents."

"Yes, he does," Brian corrected. "He knows Christmas is the spirit of giving and he has nothing to give. Except himself, and he can't give that because it belongs to you."

Brian looked sad himself.

"Clarence gives us his affection and loyalty every day of the year," I said. "There couldn't be a nicer present than that."

"Clarence would like to be like other people," Brian said, "and have something special to give at Christmas."

"Well," I said, "he's got the photographs. That nice photographer who was here for the interview sent him six prints. That's one for each of us."

Brian looked away. "I'm, ah, not sure Clarence understood those were to be Christmas presents."

"What do you mean?"

A sort of guilty look crept into Brian's face. "I had the

pictures out to wrap them about a week ago," he said, squirming slightly. "And Clarence and I were looking at them."

"So?"

"So the telephone rang and I went to answer it and by the time I got back Clarence had chewed up the pictures."

"Oh, Brian," I said. "*All* of them?"

"Well, four of them. One of the others has a corner chewed, but we thought you could have that one. You said you were going to frame yours, and the corner wouldn't show. Mother can have the undamaged one. Besides," he added, "Clarence is sorry now. He didn't realize what he was doing."

I glared at Brian. "I wasn't going to blame Clarence. You really should have put the photographs out of his reach."

"I'm sorry, too. I just didn't—" He let the sentence trail off. "But anyway, now you see why Clarence is unhappy. He has presents only for you and Mother. And he *would* like to have something else to give."

Certainly something was bothering Clarence. Maybe Brian was right. But I didn't know what we should do about it.

Then, on the morning of Christmas Eve, Clarence suddenly cheered up.

I thought it was because of the puppies. Clarence was the only one who knew I had them. Mrs. Olsen had called to say I could have the puppies any time I wanted now. So I smuggled them into the house Christmas Eve morning. I thought I would bring them out in the evening or perhaps Christmas morning. I didn't see how Mother could refuse to keep all four. They were so cute together and it would be Christmas and everyone would be feeling happy and gay. I put the puppies in the laundry room, where no one would be likely to go.

Brian thought Clarence had cheered up because of the excitement. We all went to the station to meet Uncle Jeffrey and Aunt Minnie. After that there were suitcases to unpack, mysterious bundles, and lots of chatter. Clarence had games with Uncle Jeffrey. And, because it was Christmas, Aunt Minnie had given up poking Clarence with her umbrella.

Uncle Peter remembered he was spending Christmas with us and arrived a little later. He didn't forget anyone's name or that he had invited Clarence and me to New York.

It was a very happy time. Aunt Minnie was carrying her book of useful information, but for once she didn't open it. She didn't even tell us how to trim the Christmas tree.

Uncle Jeffrey was jolly and didn't say a thing when Clarence joined in the carol singing after dinner. Clarence has a loud, clear voice, but he's not very good at following the melody.

Finally it was time to open the presents.

Clarence opened all his own presents without any help. In the excitement he also opened several that weren't his. Clarence had a new Fish, a bright red bowl, a box of dog candy. He had wanted a television set of his own, which he didn't get, but he seemed very happy with his presents. Uncle Jeffrey had given him and Brian a detective kit for

How Well trained Dogs Behave
Merry Christmas
Clarence
Aunt Minnie

tracking people. Uncle Peter had given him a plaid collar. Aunt Minnie gave Clarence a book on how well-trained dogs behave.

Clarence loved his book. It was the first one he had ever had. He laid aside Fish and took his book. He tore out a page, chewed it up, and then carefully spat out the pieces before tearing the next page. Clarence was enjoying his present more than Aunt Minnie had ever dreamed he would.

"Well, that was very nice," Aunt Minnie said when the last present had been opened. She was sitting in a chair surrounded by boxes of handkerchiefs and boxes of writing paper. Aunt Minnie has so much money that it is hard to think of what to give her for Christmas.

Clarence went into the hall and scratched at the door to the kitchen. Brian was admiring the necktie with a hand-painted picture of a horse which he had given Uncle Jeffrey. He laid it down and opened the door for Clarence. Then he went back to admiring the tie.

"I'll tell you, Brian," Uncle Jeffrey said, "if you like that tie so much, I might let you wear it from time to time."

"Would you, Uncle Jeffrey? I mean, would it be all right when I was the one who gave it to you?"

Everyone seemed so happy and contented that I thought this would be a good time to introduce the puppies. I went into the kitchen and there was Clarence waiting to get into the laundry room. When I opened the door, he rounded up the puppies and herded them into the kitchen. It's not easy to herd four lively puppies, but Clarence did it, pushing them into a group with his nose

and urging them through the kitchen. At last he got them all into the hall.

Nobody was paying any attention to us, so I stood and watched while Clarence studied his problem. Two steps lead down into our living room, and the puppies were too small to get down the steps. After a little thought, Clarence picked up one puppy by the back of its neck, carried it down himself, and laid the puppy beside Brian.

"Oh, Clarence," Brian breathed. "Is it for me?" Clarence wagged his tail. As everyone crowded closer and Brian picked up the puppy, Clarence went back into the hall.

He came trotting down the steps with another puppy. This one he gave to Uncle Jeffrey.

"I say, Clarence," said Uncle Jeffrey, "this is very handsome of you, old man." Uncle Jeffrey's hands looked strangely gentle as he picked up his puppy.

Clarence made another trip. When he came back with the third puppy, he gave it to Aunt Minnie. Or rather, he stood at her feet with it, waiting to make sure there wasn't going to be any poking with the umbrella.

Aunt Minnie laid down her umbrella. Her book slid to the floor. She leaned forward and took her puppy. Her face got all soft and smile-y.

Uncle Peter got the fourth puppy. "You know," he said, "I think a puppy is just what I need."

Now everybody had a puppy, except Mother and me. I already had a dog, of course. Mother had Brian and me. And we each had a picture of Clarence.

Clarence surveyed the scene. As soon as he saw each new owner was taking good care of his puppy, Clarence gave a big sigh and lay down on a pile of Christmas wrappings.

I looked around, too. Brian, of course, you would expect to be pleased, but I wasn't sure about Aunt Minnie and Uncle Peter and Uncle Jeffrey. I needn't have worried.

"Now I have a reason to remember what day it is and whether the next meal is breakfast or dinner," Uncle Peter said.

Aunt Minnie looked almost as if she might cry when she said, "Nobody, nobody ever gave me such a nice present before."

Uncle Jeffrey said, holding tight to his puppy, "I wonder where Clarence got them?"

"Why, they're his," Brian said, surprised the others hadn't noticed. He grinned at me to show that now he understood about Clarence's secret.

"His?" said Uncle Jeffrey.

"Well, look at them. They all look like little Clarences," Brian pointed out.

And so they did.

We turned out all the lights except those on the tree and sang "Silent Night," with Clarence putting in a few notes here and there.

As we started for bed, Aunt Minnie said, "I think I'll take my puppy with me. He might get lonesome during the night."

I thought it would be better to put the puppies with Clarence in the kitchen. But I didn't say anything because it was clear all the new dog owners thought Aunt Minnie had the right idea.

Mother came in to see me as I was getting ready for bed. "Where did the puppies come from?" she asked.

"I brought them over," I admitted. "I thought—"

"I see," Mother said. She pretended to wipe her forehead. "I guess I had a narrow escape. Five Clarences in one house might be too much of a good thing. Thank you, Clarence, for distributing the puppies."

Clarence, who was lying on the foot of my bed, wagged his tail.

I was very glad I had kept his secret.

So that was how Clarence solved his Christmas shopping problem. And that was how Brian and Uncle Jeffrey and Uncle Peter and Aunt Minnie happened to get dogs.

We haven't seen Uncle Peter for several months—since Christmas, in fact. He still wants Clarence and me to visit him and his dog, which seems to be called Jeffrey. Uncle Jeffrey is flattered that Uncle Peter named his dog that. But Uncle Jeffrey can't figure out why Uncle Peter has taken to calling *him* Wags.

Brian's dog, of course, lives right here. He is fairly well behaved because Clarence has turned out to be a strict father.

Uncle Jeffrey and Aunt Minnie bring their dogs now when they come to visit. We have never seen such undisciplined, badly trained dogs. Clarence has to correct them all the time.

Aunt Minnie leaves her umbrella and her book at home. She's much too busy looking after her dog to offer anyone else advice.

Uncle Jeffrey just laughs when his dog jumps on the

furniture, knocks over vases, and eats dog biscuits in the dining room. "You know," he said the last time he was here, "the little fellow just can't sleep anywhere but on the foot of my bed. Cries all night if I shut him out of the room. And I've had to get a television set. He does enjoy watching it. Takes after his father. I may give Clarence a TV set next Christmas."